Mike's eyes didn't leave Sherry's face.

In their velvet depths lay ecstasy. And guaranteed heartbreak.

The spark that had leapt between them earlier seemed only to intensify, causing unwanted thoughts to race through her mind. Was it her imagination, or had Mike's lips parted slightly? How would it feel if he pressed them against hers?

She had to get hold of herself. Stop regarding Mike as forbidden fruit and think of him as a source of income for her fatherless nephew. She would cultivate a personal relationship with the man—indulge in a flirtation, if necessary. But she had her principles.

She positively wouldn't share his bed.

Still, an involuntary shiver of anticipation knifed clear through Sherry's virginal soul....

Dear Reader,

Babies—who can resist them? Celebrating the wonder of new life—and new love—Silhouette Romance introduces a brand-new series, BUNDLES OF JOY. In these wonderful stories, couples are brought together by babies—and kept together by love! We hope you enjoy all six BUNDLES OF JOY books in April. Look for more in the months to come.

Favorite author Suzanne Carey launches the series with *The Daddy Project*. Sherry Tompkins is caring for her infant nephew and she needs help from the child's father, Mike Ruiz. Is marrying Mike the best way to find out if he's daddy material?

Lindsay Longford brings us *The Cowboy, the Baby and the Runaway Bride*. T. J. Tyler may have been left at the altar years ago by Callie Jo Murphy, but now this rugged cowboy and his adorable baby boy are determined to win her back.

Lullaby and Goodnight is a dramatic new story from Sandra Steffen about a single mom on the run. LeAnna Chadwick longs to stay in the shelter of Vince Macelli's arms, but the only way to protect her child is to leave the man she loves.

The excitement continues with *Adam's Vow*, Karen Rose Smith's book about one man's search for his missing daughters—and the beautiful, mysterious woman who helps him. Love and laughter abound in Pat Montana's *Babies Inc.*, a tale of two people who go into the baby business together and find romance in the process. And debut author Christine Scott brings us the heartwarming *Hazardous Husband*.

I hope you will enjoy BUNDLES OF JOY. Until next month—

Happy Reading!

Anne Canadeo
Senior Editor
Silhouette Romance

Please address questions and book requests to:
Silhouette Reader Service
U.S.: 3010 Walden Ave., P.O. Box 1325, Buffalo, NY 14269
Canadian: P.O. Box 609, Fort Erie, Ont. L2A 5X3

Suzanne Carey

THE DADDY PROJECT

Silhouette
ROMANCE™
Published by Silhouette Books
America's Publisher of Contemporary Romance

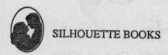

SILHOUETTE BOOKS

RECYCLED PAPER

ISBN 0-373-19072-7

THE DADDY PROJECT

Books by Suzanne Carey

Silhouette Romance

A Most Convenient Marriage #633
Run, Isabella #682
Virgin Territory #736
The Baby Contract #777
Home for Thanksgiving #825
Navajo Wedding #855
Baby Swap #880
Dad Galahad #928
Marry Me Again #1001
The Male Animal #1025
The Daddy Project #1072

Silhouette Desire

Kiss and Tell #4
Passion's Portrait #69
Mountain Memory #92
Leave Me Never #126
Counterparts #176
Angel in His Arms #206
Confess to Apollo #268
Love Medicine #310
Any Pirate in a Storm #368

Silhouette Intimate Moments

Never Say Goodbye #330
Strangers When We Meet #392
True to the Fire #435
Eleanora's Ghost #518

Silhouette Books

Silhouette Summer Sizzlers 1993
"Steam Bath"

SUZANNE CAREY

is a former reporter and magazine editor who prefers to write romance novels because they add to the sum total of love in the world.

Bundles of JOY

Dear Readers,

As the author who created him—and thus his "mother," in a sense—I was privileged to share the emotions that buffeted Mike Ruiz, the hero of *The Daddy Project*, when he learned that Jamie was his son—flesh of his flesh, heir to his dark eyes, the bearer of his genes. What a rush of fatherly love and protectiveness—along with bitter memories of the past—swept him after his astonishing discovery.

I had a bit longer to get used to the idea of being a parent before my first "bundle of joy," my daughter Nancy, arrived—four weeks early. But in no sense was I truly prepared for the profound sense of wonder and connectedness to past and future generations her coming would evoke. As I held my little preemie for the first time— all five pounds, fourteen ounces of her—I realized she wasn't quite "finished." In the rush to arrive and be my little girl, she hadn't bothered to wait for eyelashes! Yet she was perfect in every detail.

In the course of time, Nancy acquired two sisters. Each time, for me, the awe and mystery of bonding with my new baby was the same. In loving and raising a child, it seems to me, we who are fortunate enough to become parents express most deeply who we are, yet rise most weightlessly beyond the boundaries of our human isolation and selfishness.

Sincerely,

Suzanne Carey

Chapter One

Finally, after months of catching an occasional glimpse of him on the evening news and reading about his exploits in her morning paper, Sherry Tompkins would see Mike Ruiz in person. Gaze into the allegedly mesmerizing eyes of the man who'd impregnated and dumped her late half sister, Lisa. And begin the process of deciding whether he had what it took to be a fit parent.

Her chin thrust forward slightly to compensate for the jitters she felt over the plan she'd conceived to check him out, Sherry elbowed her way through the crush of university professors, social science students, news junkies and assorted community activists who were crowding into an already packed auditorium at the University of South Florida in Tampa to hear him speak.

As she did so, a buzz of excitement filled the air, causing her to purse her lips. Thanks to his high-profile campaign to improve the lot of migrant farmworkers throughout Florida and the southeast, the man she'd come to see had become something of a hero. His tactics—boycotts, picketing, silver-tongued persuasion, hardball politics and masterful use of the media—were said to be much admired by advocates of the downtrodden. Women in particular found it easy to love him. Or so she'd heard. When they spoke of him, even hard-bitten female reporters tended to gush.

Thanks to the story Lisa had confided to her during the final months of her pregnancy, Sherry had a vastly different opinion of him. I'd give anything if we didn't have to meet, she thought. I'll find it galling just to be civil to him.

A moment later, she spotted an unoccupied seat near the middle of the second row. Managing to claim it before someone else could, she smoothed her shining, chin-length cap of gold-brown hair into place and settled back to wait. She didn't have much choice and, in a way, that made things easier. She'd *have* to confront him if she could.

In essence, it was a question of money, that bugaboo of the Hayes-Tompkins clan for as long as Sherry could remember. Home again after graduating *cum laude* with a business degree from the University of Florida in Gainesville, she'd all but exhausted her slender resources getting an education, so that she could pursue her dream of working as a tax accountant. Whatever she'd had left after paying for tuition, books, food and shelter, she'd contributed to Jamie's upkeep. If she didn't find a job, and soon, she'd be scraping the last dollar from her bank account.

Like Sherry, Lillian Hayes, her seventy-six-year-old grandmother, was strapped for cash. Yet she'd uncomplainingly paid the balance of little Jamie's expenses out of her monthly Social Security check in addition to acting as his full-time nursemaid since Lisa's death from a ruptured aneurysm when he was two months old. Lately, the strain had begun to tell on her. For years, she'd suffered from rheumatoid arthritis and diabetes. Now, according to her doctor, the diabetes was getting worse. She needed to watch her diet more closely and get adequate rest.

Meanwhile, Jamie was getting to be a handful. All boy and thoroughly adorable with the big, dark eyes and saucy grin Mike Ruiz had doubtlessly contributed to his genetic makeup, Sherry's eleven-month-old nephew had been crawling for quite some time. Soon, he'd be walking and getting into everything. It would be a full-time job just running after him, one better suited to someone Sherry's age. Ironically, if she found work, she wouldn't be able to help out much. Reliable day care was the only answer. And that cost the kind of money she wouldn't earn for several years yet.

A lawyer capable of earning a decent living, the boy's father could and should make up the difference. It was only right. Yet Sherry had hesitated to contact him. Once he saw Jamie, Mike Ruiz might change his mind about being a father and want shared custody or visitation rights in return for his support. She had to be sure his presence in her nephew's life would be a positive one before risking that possibility.

Ironically, though she disliked Jamie's father without ever having set eyes on him, that presence was her second goal. Beginning with her grandmother, the Hayes family chronicle had been one of husbandless women and fatherless children. The former Lillian McVey's father had been shot in a tavern brawl when she was three. Fourteen years later, she'd married Roy Hayes, an alcoholic who'd deserted her when their daughter, Ruth, was just a baby.

The family history had continued to go downhill from there. Sherry's mother, Ruth Hayes Tompkins, hadn't married Lisa's father, though she'd tied the knot with Sherry's before Sherry was born. Tragically, both Ruth and her husband had been killed in a car accident during the only vacation they'd ever taken. Lillian had been left to raise Lisa and Sherry on her own.

By itself, watching and listening to the charismatic, dark-haired activist who'd fathered Jamie hold forth about the injustices suffered by migrant laborers wouldn't be enough for Sherry to form a judgement. She regarded it simply as a starting place, a serendipitous chance to observe him unawares before arriving at his Kennedy Boulevard office that afternoon and interviewing for the job his organization, the Florida Farmworkers' Union, had advertised.

Reluctant as she was to meet and interact with her sister's despoiler, Sherry viewed the announcement she'd spotted in a local paper as a godsend. If she could persuade Mike Ruiz to hire her, she'd get a close-up look at how he handled himself. Observe him on good days and bad. Actively listen to the office gossip about his love life. And see how he treated people who were subordinate to him.

The ad had simply stated FFU's need to fill an open position and invited qualified applicants to apply. She doubted the job would pay very much, but that hardly mattered to her. If Mike Ruiz hired her, she'd report to work for a maximum of two weeks. In that much time, she ought to be able to come to a decision.

She wasn't worried about being chosen if someone else hadn't beaten her to the punch. A former manicurist who'd subsidized her first two years of college by applying and maintaining artificial fingernails at a local beauty shop, she'd attended secretarial school before beginning her studies at the university, and worked part-time as secretary to the business dean in Gainesville. She was capable of taking flawless shorthand and typing ninety words a minute. To improve her chances, she might admit to having taken a "few classes." But she didn't plan to arouse Mike Ruiz's suspicions about her motives by confessing to a bachelor's degree....

Her train of thought interrupted by a lull in the auditorium as the skinny, bespectacled student who would present the guest speaker approached the microphone, Sherry firmed up her resolve. What she planned to do might not be strictly honest. But it was *right* in a broader sense. She had little Jamie's welfare to think about.

Mercifully for the keyed-up state of her psyche, the student master of ceremonies kept his introduction brief. A moment later, Mike Ruiz was striding onto the stage with a confident grace to wildly enthusiastic applause.

The snapshot of him Lisa had retained and shared with her hadn't prepared Sherry for the man himself. Overcome by a rush of some ill-defined emotion, she was forced to admit that, on the surface, at least, he was everything Lisa had claimed. It wasn't difficult to see why her sister had fallen for him.

Medium-tall and less-than-handsome in the traditional sense, possessed of a compact, muscular build, charmingly irregular features and a wry, self-deprecating grin that flashed winningly against the coppery suntan of his complexion, Mike Ruiz radiated self-confidence and physical appeal. His thick, dark hair—neatly trimmed in a youthful cut—shone like the pelt of a healthy animal. Beguiled for a hot second into imagining its texture beneath her fingertips, Sherry hastily banished the notion. His eyes are his best feature, she decided grudgingly as he scanned the audience with the clear expectation that, for him, their interchange would be a gratifying one. Like Jamie's, they were big and dark, fringed with long, straight, lashes. They shone with an immense capacity for willfulness and delight. From what she could tell, the resemblance to his baby son didn't stop there. Despite his tender age, Jamie was a stalwart little character, ready to fling himself into any adventure that beckoned. Asked to describe his personality, the essence of his budding self, Sherry would have said without hesitation that the boy had "heart."

It was an attribute Lisa had lacked, despite her many good qualities. Now, as Sherry stared at her sister's partner in creating the little boy she held increasingly dear, she speculated it might have come from him. Irresponsible womanizer and deadbeat dad though she believed him to be, there was something gallant, even praiseworthy about the way Mike Ruiz dared to challenge Florida's powerful agribusiness establishment and political elite on behalf of the downtrodden and voiceless. She wanted to like him despite herself.

It wasn't going to happen. When it came to his charisma, she'd been innoculated. As he motioned for quiet and began his speech by asking members of the audience to volunteer their ethnic heritage, she reminded herself with painful pragmatism of the course Lisa's romance with him had taken.

She and Mike Ruiz had met playing pool in a bar, her sister had told her. And started to date. Before long, she'd been sleeping over at his South Westshore apartment on a regular basis.

"Then I got pregnant and he didn't want anything further to do with me." Lisa had grimaced with an ironic twist of her red-lipsticked mouth, pushing back a limp strand of hair from her forehead and morosely cradling her swollen belly through a faded print wrapper as the two of them had rocked together on their grandmother's porch a month before Jamie's birth. "The fact is, he dumped me. I know what you're thinking, Sher. And you're probably right. I should make him pay through the nose. Fortunately for him, I'm too proud to ask that expletive-deleted for anything."

I'm not too proud, Sherry thought as she watched Mike Ruiz collect answers ranging from England, Ireland and Poland to Lebanon, Cuba and Vietnam. There's nothing shameful about asking a man to take responsibility for his behavior. Completing his informal survey, Mike paused for impact, making roving eye contact with individual members of his audience. As he did so, his gaze met Sherry's, moved on, then returned and hesitated for a fraction of a second. Do I know her? he asked himself with a slight frown. There's something familiar about her face, though I can't quite place it. Maybe it's the shape of her jaw. Or the curve of her mouth. Yet he was positive they'd never met. She was one classy woman—the kind he'd almost certainly have remembered.

"Thanks for helping me make a point I wanted to make...namely that, unless our ancestors were Native American, most of us can trace our heritage to foreign countries," he resumed, glancing away. "Like several of you, I trace mine to Cuba. Yet I was born here. I grew up taking America's blessings for granted. Like the right to fair treatment, decent housing, a living wage...things the itinerant laborers from Mexico, Haiti and Central America who pick our fruit and vegetables may or may not have accorded to them..."

As he segued into the body of his speech, an eloquent plea for money, volunteers and people willing to contact their state legislators on behalf of a migrant-aid bill he favored, Sherry found herself picturing the details of her sister's affair with him. Unlike Lisa, who'd begun her amorous career at sixteen in the back of a pickup truck, Sherry was still a virgin at twenty-seven. She had to fill in the blanks with her imagination.

Lamentably for her peace of mind, it was all too easy to envision what he'd be like in bed. And guess how painful their parting had been for her sister. According to Lisa, the sexy Cuban-American lawyer/activist had set her on her heels. Falling for him had caused her to mend her ways, rethink where she was headed. She'd longed to settle down. Get married. Have a child with him. Ironically, she'd gotten *part* of what she'd wanted.

Running like a parallel stream through her dead sister's remembered confidences was Sherry's assessment of the man she'd come to evaluate. Tough, outspoken and brilliant, ostensibly warmhearted, he was—on the surface—the sort of man who attracted her. Remember Lisa, penniless and pregnant, pouring out her anguish on Gram's front porch, she reproached herself. Remember Jamie, whose father brushed aside his existence like a gnat. It won't be difficult to stay goal-oriented.

At last Mike Ruiz's speech and the question-and-answer period that followed it were over. Mobbed by reporters and well-wishers, he began to make his way out of the auditorium. Risking the possibility he'd notice and remember her, Sherry stayed close.

He loves a crowd, she thought disparagingly. Especially the women. And why wouldn't he, the way they fawn over him? Take that female reporter from Channel 11. I wouldn't give two cents for her objectivity. If she got any closer with that microphone, she'd be shoving it down his throat.

Feeling confident and happy as he traded good-natured jibes with Mary Murchison, acknowledged glamor girl of WTPA's six o'clock news, Mike felt the weight of Sherry's gaze. Turning his head partway, he glanced in her direction. As he did so, his pupils widened, all but swallowing up the lively dark brown of his irises. The vibes he'd responded to so intuitively had come from the tawny-haired young woman he'd noticed earlier, near the beginning of his speech. A lone wolf in the romance department since he and Lisa Hayes had parted company eighteen months earlier, he felt something click even though she wasn't the type that usually appealed to him.

Slender, small-breasted, her gamine features only sparingly enhanced with makeup, she wore a short-sleeved cotton blouse and narrow madras plaid skirt that stopped at her kneecaps. Despite the unbecoming height of her neatly polished, flat-heeled shoes, her slim, shapely legs seemed to go on forever like those of a highly paid model. With a flicker of eroticism he acknowledged was totally inappropriate to the moment, he imagined her wrapping them about his waist.

Even more intriguing was the discovery that her appeal transcended the physical. He was equally charmed by the spark of determination in her clear, gray eyes, her unmistakable air of independence. Though there was something vulnerable about her as well, a kind of softness that aroused his protective instincts, he sensed she had it firmly in check. He had a wildly inexplicable notion that something more complex than simple man-woman chemistry had drawn them to each other.

"Should I know you?" he mouthed through the crush of bodies that separated them.

It was the kind of invitation to flirt that Sherry had rebuffed a hundred times and never given a second thought. This time, it struck terror in her heart. Transfixed like a deer in the headlights of a sixteen-wheeler, she wanted to run for her life. Although he had to pay for what he'd done to her sister, to her consternation, the primitive woman in Sherry was thoroughly intrigued with him.

Panic-stricken that he should catch her in the act of sizing him up before their interview had even taken place, she shook her head. Before he could make his way toward her, she'd vanished into the crowd as she made a beeline for the door.

She doesn't like me, Mike realized to his surprise. I wonder why. We're strangers to each other.

Hector Machado, his close friend and second in command at FFU, chose that moment to place a restraining hand on his arm. "Don't forget, Miguelito... we're supposed to stop by Rudy K.'s," he said. "Plus, you got an interview with some woman who wants to be your secretary."

But Mike felt his time would be better served by checking out a complaint from some Salvadorans in Thonotosassa about unsanitary living conditions. "*You* go butter up Rudy," he told his friend impatiently, "and interview that woman. I've got more important things to worry about."

* * *

Parking in front of her grandmother's shabby rental house in the city's historic if somewhat rundown Port Tampa section, Sherry turned off the ignition and sat quietly behind the wheel of her beige compact for a moment. She was still reeling from her encounter with Mike Ruiz. If she went into the house without taking a second to calm herself first, Gram would know something was up. She'd guess—rightly—that it involved Sherry's plan to wring child support from Mike after checking him out, and warn her for the umpteenth time that it would be a mistake.

"The Hayes family has made it without help from outsiders or goin' on welfare for six generations," she'd say. "And we can keep on makin' it. I ain't so old and sick I can't do my part."

When Sherry walked into the house, she found her grandmother asleep on the sunporch in front of the television. Gurgling to himself in his playpen as he banged on his jack-in-the-box with a plastic spoon, Jamie needed a diaper change. Though he wasn't complaining yet, it was also past time for him to eat.

"You're a patient little guy, did you know that?" Sherry praised her nephew as she scooped him up. "You deserve the best in life, and I'm going to see that you get it."

In response, Jamie pulled her hair, laughing with delight at her exaggerated "Ouch!" as she pried his dimpled fingers from its silken strands.

Kissing his cheek and thinking how deeply she'd learned to love him now that she was back in Tampa and could participate in his care on a daily basis, she carried the boy into the living room and changed him on the sofa, applying a light dusting of cornstarch, which was cheaper than baby powder. He was Lisa's son. Yet it was almost as if she'd given birth to him. Irrational or not, her fear that Mike Ruiz would demand full-time custody in return for his financial support grew as the bond between her and her nephew strengthened.

I wish we had another choice, she thought, fastening Jamie's diaper tabs as her grandmother's light snores floated toward her through the open doorway. The fact is, we don't. There's no money for day care. And Gram isn't capable of watching him anymore, despite her protestations.

Clearly pleased by the clean, comfortable feeling her ministrations had evoked, Jamie waved his legs in the air and beamed at a quick game of patty-cake. Absolutely everything about him was precious, from his exquisitely formed toes to the creases in his chubby thighs and the perfect half-moons of his fingernails. In her opinion, he was a flawless human being possessed of amazing talents and a heart brimming with love. How could a man who seemed to care so much about the fate of strangers have taken so little interest in his own child?

Remember to ask yourself that question whenever you're tempted to daydream about how sexy he is or excuse his culpability, she thought with a wry twist of her mouth. Remember Lisa and what she went through. Remember your little nephew.

On the sunporch, the day's installment of her grandmother's favorite soap opera continued to unfold as the older woman slept. Meanwhile, Sherry had forty-five minutes or so before she had to get back in her car and drive to FFU headquarters for her interview. And Jamie needed some lap time.

"Come on, sweetheart ... let's eat," she invited, hoisting the boy on her hip and carrying him into the kitchen.

Jamie's midday meal consisted of baby spaghetti and meat sauce, followed by several spoonfuls of pureed plums for dessert. When his bottle had warmed sufficently that the milk's temperature felt neutral on the inside of her wrist, she took him back into the living room. Settling into an overstuffed chair with him in her arms, she offered it to him. Though he could hold his bottle by himself with ease, Jamie sometimes preferred that someone else do the honors. His bright, intelligent eyes remained fixed on her face as he nursed, making it seem that, like her, he felt their strong mother-and-child connection.

She was very nearly late for her appointment. Jamie had cried when she'd put him back in his playpen and it had awakened her grandmother. She'd had to comfort him and listen respectfully to the warning she'd hoped to avoid. It was two minutes to 3:00 p.m. when she walked into FFU's storefront office, which had been converted from a failed sandwich shop in a blighted block west of the downtown.

Its decor was early Goodwill. In addition to a trio of battered desks and a wall lined with filing cabinets, it featured a toy bin, a row of less-than-pristine waiting room chairs, several blackboards and a huge stack of folding chairs that looked as if they'd seen many years of service. Every available vertical space was covered with a thick layer of bulletins and posters. The reception desk wasn't manned. Ringing the bell as a hand-lettered placard directed, she waited. The man she'd been steeling herself to meet didn't materialize. Instead, a chunky Hispanic a few years his senior emerged from one of the inner offices wiping the remains of a sandwich from his chin. He eyed her speculatively. "I'm Hector Machado," he said after a moment. "You must be Sherry Tompkins. Please...have a seat. Tell me about your qualifications."

They faced each other across the reception desk. She'd brought a neatly typed résumé and, for starters, she handed it to him. His brows lifted slightly as he perused it. "Ninety words a minute plus shorthand, huh?" he asked. "Plus you speak some Spanish. I'm impressed. How come you wanna work here, anyway?"

She realized she'd been right not to mention her degree. It wasn't the sort of job for a college graduate. Anyway, given the rock-bottom salary they were offering, she might have submitted the only application.

"For one thing, it's close to home," she answered. "I have a year-old son and—"

A note of skepticism crept into Hector's voice as he interrupted her. "We need somebody reliable, Miss Tompkins. Or is it Missus? You got a friend or relative, maybe, to look after him?"

"It's *Miss.* Actually, my grandmother—"

Just then, the glass door to the street opened and Mike breezed in. His Thonotosassa complaint hadn't amounted to much and he was running early. He did a double take when he saw Sherry in the visitor's chair.

"*You!*" he exclaimed, effortlessly re-establishing the link between them that had so upset her earlier. "What are you doing here? You're the girl I saw at USF."

Sherry struggled to collect herself. At close range, he was even sexier than she'd realized. Tugged into responding, she resisted. The time had come to prove her mettle.

"No... the *woman,*" she answered. "I'm here about the job."

Mike realized she wasn't going to pretend nothing had happened between them—merely that it hadn't amounted to much, insofar as she was concerned. So, what had she been doing at his speech?

He'd find out soon enough. Meantime, he gave a low whistle. "Just what we need around here," he said with mock sarcasm. "A radical feminist!"

Sherry shrugged. She imagined her casual attitude would have greatly amused her dead sister. "Maybe. If you don't have any other candidates..."

The fact was, they didn't. Mike grinned. "We'll have to hire you."

"That sounds logical."

"Well... carry on."

Her interview with Hector continued, with Mike hanging around a minute or two before disappearing into his private office. Like Sherry, Hector seemed to relax a little at his departure.

"Okay, Miss Tompkins," he said. "Your résumé looks good. Though we didn't ask for shorthand, it'll come in handy. How about taking a couple of paragraphs' worth of dictation, and typing 'em up?"

Removing a notebook and pencil from her purse, Sherry indicated her willingness. The excerpt from a magazine he dictated at a moderate speed turned out to be child's play. She reproduced it effortlessly after first checking to see whether any of the keys on the ancient typewriter he pointed out had a habit of sticking. She had done her best.

Almost apologetically, Hector informed her that Mike had the final say. She'd have to talk with him before being put on the payroll. Bracing herself for her intense reaction to his pheromones, not to mention several probing questions, she allowed his assistant to usher her into the lion's den.

In the midst of a phone conversation, Mike waved her to a seat. For the most part, he seemed to be listening to someone, though now and then he interjected a "yeah," or an "okay," accompanied by a brief, emphatic nod of his head. Once or twice, he raked his fingers absently through his thick, dark hair. As he did so, his eyes didn't leave her face. "Who are you, anyway?" they seemed to be asking her. "Are we destined to mean something to each other?"

In their velvet depths lay ecstasy. And danger. Guaranteed heartbreak, or so her sister had intimated. Now her own experience with him was unfolding and it had her by the throat. The spark that had leapt between them in the crowded foyer following his speech seemed only to intensify, causing all manner of unwanted thoughts to race through her head. Was it her imagination, or had his lips parted slightly? How would it feel if he pressed them against her throat?

Somehow, she had to get hold of herself. Stop regarding him as forbidden fruit and think of him as a source of income for her nephew. If necessary, she'd cultivate a personal relationship with him. But she wouldn't share his bed. Or indulge in anything more serious than a flirtation. She had her principles, after all—her loyalties to think about.

Despite them, an involuntary shiver of anticipation knifed through her as he said goodbye and returned the receiver to its cradle. To her credit, she didn't let it show. Hector had attached a note to her résumé and she waited with outward composure as he read it and returned his eyes to her face.

"Can you really type with those?" he asked in Spanish, nodding at her fingernails, which were long, shapely and carefully lacquered with rose nail enamel.

A bit too personal, the curveball question relaxed her a little. If he thought he'd rattle her by conducting the interview in Spanish, he had another think coming. She gave him a diffident smile. "I really can," she said. "The fact is, I'm used to them. You probably noticed on my résumé I was a manicurist before I went to secretarial school."

"Tell me why you want this job."

"That's easy. I need the money. My grandmother is elderly and I have—"

"Are you married or involved with anyone?"

"I don't see how that's pertinent."

Something flickered in his gaze. "Okay," he said. "I won't tread on that. Let's talk about something else. Tell me how you feel about itinerant farmworkers. Do they deserve fair treatment under the law? What if they aren't U.S. citizens?"

Abruptly they were conversing on neutral ground and she found she could talk to him. "All people deserve to be treated fairly...no matter *who* they are," she replied. "You might think that, coming from a poor family as I do, I'd feel a sense of competitiveness with migrants for jobs and social standing. But I don't. In my opinion, there's room in this country for all of us to better ourselves."

She wasn't anybody's fool. More to the point, from his perspective, her heart was in the right place. "So do I, Miss Tompkins," he said, flashing his faintly lopsided grin. "You're hired. Now... how about taking a letter to the Hillsborough County Commission? And one to the governor's office?"

If only he wasn't so likable, she thought. It would be easier to hate him. Taking out her notebook, she jotted down his remarks as quickly as she could and got to her feet. "Is there anything else?" she asked.

Mike stood also. "Actually, yes." His tone was vaguely apologetic. "Any chance you can be available to take notes at a meeting tonight? It's in Lakeland. You'll be paid overtime, of course."

If she hesitated before answering, it wasn't because of Jamie. Gram could watch him for a little while yet. "Lakeland's a fairly long haul," she pointed out. "And my car needs work. I'm leery about taking it on the highway after dark."

"No problem," Mike answered, hating himself for rejoicing in her automotive troubles. "We can ride over together."

Her purpose was getting to know him, wasn't it? Well, this was her chance. "All right," she agreed. "I'll just phone my grandmother and let her know I'll be late."

Mike asked Sherry to send in Hector when she returned to the outer office. Accordingly, she had the place to herself as she phoned Gram and typed his letters. There were several calls for Mike, all of minor importance, in her judgement, and she took messages. She was just finishing the second letter when Hector reappeared, heading for the door.

Pausing beside her desk, he cleared his throat. "I just wanna say... congratulations on being hired, Miss Tompkins. I hope you like it here."

His good wishes made her feel less than ethical. "Call me Sherry," she answered, regretful she had to operate under false premises with him, as well. "Thanks for giving me a good recommendation."

Following his departure, she foraged around for envelopes and sat back down at the typewriter. A short time later, she was rapping lightly on Mike's door and entering without waiting for an invitation from him. He wasn't at his desk and, briefly, she thought he'd slipped out a back exit.

Then she realized where he was. Naked to the waist, he was standing before the sink in his private bath, washing the day's accumulation of sweat and grime from his upper body. To her consternation, his unadorned torso was magnificent. Rooted to the spot, she felt compelled to follow its downward-pointing seam of coarse, dark hair with her eyes to where it disappeared beneath the waistband of his trousers.

The power of her physical reaction to his partial nudity left her feeling as if she'd been punched in the stomach. To counteract it, she forced herself to picture him making love to her sister. Impregnating Lisa. And subsequently abandoning her. To her horror, she felt a twinge of jealousy.

For his part, caught off guard and rendered immobile by the expression on Sherry's face, Mike was buffeted by a kaleidoscope of wildly conflicting emotions. Strongly attracted to her from the moment they'd met, and half convinced she felt the same way, he was on the verge of getting an erection. At the same time, he felt as if he'd offended her. Yet he hadn't *done* anything.

"Look," he said awkwardly, reaching for a towel and wishing it was a bathrobe, or maybe a tent. "I should have warned you... I sometimes wash up and change my shirt when I have an evening appointment."

Shaky and barely audible, Sherry's reply seemed to stick in her throat. "There's...no need to apologize," she whispered. "I'm the one who walked in on you."

He shrugged. "No harm done."

I'm not so sure about that, Sherry thought. I have to live with myself. "I'll just put this stuff on your desk," she managed to say in a more normal tone. "And wait for you in the outer office."

Chapter Two

Sherry had herself fairly well in hand by the time Mike emerged in a clean shirt and tie along with the darkly conservative suit jacket and trousers he'd worn earlier. Nevertheless, she did her best to avoid direct eye contact with him. It was safer that way, in her opinion. Each time their gaze met, she might be tempted to picture him shirtless. All sorts of unwelcome thoughts might drift through her head. After the way he'd sensed her interest in a crowded hallway at the university and turned to glance in her direction, she couldn't afford to take the chance that he'd pick up on them.

To her relief, they wouldn't be traveling to Lakeland alone. Without bothering to announce his intentions in advance, Mike stopped to pick up his sister Sandra and Hector at their respective West Tampa abodes before pointing his vintage Mustang convertible toward Lakeland on Interstate 4 eastbound. Unfortunately, their presence in the back seat and the three-way conversation that resulted didn't ease her discomfort much.

For one thing, Mike had kept the top up and switched on the air-conditioning. Though her hair stayed neat and she was grateful for that, the closed car became for her a rolling cocoon of intimacy, one in which it was all too easy to feel the tug of his sensuality and respond to it. Try though she would, she couldn't seem to keep from observing the way his thigh muscles tensed and released beneath the fabric of his trouser leg each time he adjusted his pressure on the gas pedal. Or noticing the subtle, musky aroma of his after-shave, which he'd doubtless reapplied after washing up.

Each subtly telegraphed message that here was a man who could make her want to jettison her spinsterhood was like a dig in her solar plexis. Concurrently, imagined scenes from Lisa's affair with him jeered in her head.

You don't have to look. Or drink in his scent so avidly if you don't want to, she admonished herself, running the risk that their companions would think her standoffish as she turned and gazed out the window. You'd be crazy to let one awkward incident set the tone for your association with him. Thinking about Lisa, on the other hand, was salutary. If she kept doing that, there wasn't a snowball's chance in hell she'd end up as one of his conquests.

They arrived in Lakeland at the height of rush hour—somewhat early, since their meeting wasn't scheduled to start until 7:00 p.m. As it turned out, Mike had planned things that way.

"We have to eat," he pointed out reasonably, turning down a side street next to a defunct bottling plant. "That being the case, there's a terrific Mexican restaurant two doors from the agency where the meeting will be held." He flashed his infectious grin at Sherry. "They have terrific *chalupas*, in case you've never tasted one." Moments later, they were parking in front of Tio Pepe's Blue Heaven Café, a modest but scrupulously clean establishment that boasted south-of-the-border travel posters and red leatherette-upholstered booths. Determined to sit across from Mike rather than next to him so their shoulders wouldn't brush, Sherry made a point of sliding in beside Hector, leaving Mike and his sister to appropriate the bench across from them.

At once she realized her mistake. For one thing, Mike couldn't seem to keep from bumping his knees into hers. For another, the eye contact she'd been avoiding became mandatory unless she wanted him to ask if something was bothering her.

Graciously helping her negotiate the menu, which was hand-written and offered a bewildering array of unfamiliar terms, Mike suggested the *chalupas* plus an *ensalada* and a *postre* of caramel-glazed flan "made exactly as it is in Mexico." Naturally, since she'd come along on a work assignment, she needn't worry about the cost. He'd pick up the check.

The waitress, who'd greeted him effusively when they'd walked in the door, brought nacho chips and salsa first, along with soft drinks for everyone. Their entrees quickly followed—plentiful, steaming hot and spicy beyond belief. Engrossed in the mouth-searing pleasure of eating hers, Sherry almost forgot her antagonism toward Lisa's despoiler, only to have it hit her in the face like a ton of bricks when she finished eating and glanced up to find him regarding her with a thoughtful expression.

A woman could drown in those eyes, Sherry thought. Lisa did. Steeling herself against their come-hither appeal, she almost missed Sandra Ruiz's question.

"Did you grow up in Tampa?" Mike's sister had asked. "Or are you from somewhere else, like most Floridians?"

For Sherry, the offhand request for information was a powder keg. The more Mike knew about her, she believed, the more likely he'd be to put two and two together and figure out her connection to Lisa. That is, he would if he bothered to give his cast-off lover and the mother of his child a second thought.

The truth, told sparingly, was probably her best defense. "Believe it or not, I'm from around here," she confessed.

"What part of town?" The question was Mike's, and he asked it with a certain intensity, as if trying to place her from a prior meeting.

A bit easier in her chosen role, thanks in part to the good company as well as her spicy meal, Sherry shrugged. "No special part. We moved around a lot."

That's putting it mildly, she thought as he motioned for the check. With two motherless granddaughters to raise and an inadequate income, to say the least, from her part-time work as a nurse's aid at a local hospital, Lillian Hayes had been forced to change addresses each time their rent was raised. Until she'd turned sixty-five and become eligible for Social Security benefits, the progression had been mostly a downhill one. Sherry had attended nearly a dozen different schools by her sixteenth birthday. A bit of a dreamer and shyer than her older sister, she'd found it difficult to form lasting friendships. She didn't want that kind of childhood for Jamie if it could be helped.

The meeting at which she'd been asked to take notes would be held at the storefront office of the Self-Help Coalition for Spanish-Speaking Residents, a Lakeland-based consortium of agencies that served the local Hispanic population. Similar to those of Mike's advocacy group in many respects, its quarters were somewhat smaller and even more shabbily furnished. Explaining that she needn't transcribe every word, but rather could use her own judgment about the relative importance of the various participants' remarks, Mike held out a chair for her at one end of the cafeteria-style conference table.

Sandra Ruiz, a social worker at a women's crisis center on Tampa's south side who'd tagged along to learn more about similar programs in Polk County, promptly slid into the vacant place next to hers. "Mike tells me you know Spanish," she said. "Where did you learn it?"

Resolved to keep her personal history private until she'd completed the task she'd set for herself, Sherry took the question in her stride. "Various places," she murmured, getting out her pen and stenographer's notebook. "As I mentioned earlier, we moved around a lot. Some of the neighborhoods where we landed were Spanish-speaking."

Seemingly unaware that her brother's new secretary was being less than forthcoming, Sandra gave her a friendly smile. "That's the best way to learn a language, " she said. "Just the same, feel free to call on me if you find yourself questioning something. The more recent arrivals in this country tend to talk very rapidly...particularly when they're articulating strong emotions."

The meeting got under way a few minutes later and, as Sandra had warned, much of the discussion was in Spanish. Occasionally it grew heated. Several of the participants rattled off their comments like machine-gun fire. Still, though she turned to Mike's sister occasionally for confirmation of a word or phrase, Sherry was able to carry out her assignment without much difficulty. The more I do this, the easier it'll become, she thought with satisfaction as the coalition's director called for a fifteen-minute break. And then reminded herself of a very important point. The job wasn't destined to last. She'd better get that straight.

During the break, she and Sandra chatted over cans of soda in the coalition's kitchen while Mike and Hector huddled with several of the organization's board members. As they talked about various things—including Sandra's fiancé and her wedding plans—she discovered she liked Mike's sister quite a bit. Not to be blamed for her brother's actions, Sandra was Jamie's aunt, too...and just the sort of friend Sherry hoped to make, now that she was back in Tampa on a more permanent basis.

With the thought came the realization that she wasn't checking out Mike in a vacuum. Other people would be affected, people who'd accepted her at face value, liked and trusted her. They might feel hoodwinked, even abused when her objective came to light. Similarly, when she revealed her connection to Lisa, Mike might feel as if he'd been duped. If visitation or custody of Jamie became his aim, he might decide to seek it vindictively—maybe even to use his legal expertise to wrest the boy completely from her and her grandmother.

I can't let that happen, Sherry thought. Jamie deserves to know both sides of his family. And we'd be devastated without him. If she judged Mike capable of parenting the boy, she'd have to make him see that her motives had been unselfish ones.

Following the meeting, which broke up shortly after 11:00 p.m., Mike drove Hector and his sister home before returning Sherry to her car. It wasn't long until they were pulling to the curb behind it, outside his Kennedy Boulevard office.

"Well...thanks for the ride," Sherry said, wishing him a polite 'good evening' as she reached for the door handle.

She almost jumped out of her skin when he laid a restraining hand on her arm. *Please...don't!* her eyes beseeched.

It was dark inside the Mustang and he didn't seem to notice. "It's fairly late," he noted. "And, as you say, your car's been acting up. Maybe I'd better follow you home."

Strained by the sensations that flowed from his touch, Sherry tried to dissent. He wouldn't let her get by with it. "I'd feel responsible if anything happened to you," he reiterated.

Concession appeared to offer her only escape. "All right, if you insist, though it isn't really necessary," she acquiesced, thanking her lucky stars that she and Lillian Hayes had moved shortly before Jamie's birth. Their current address wouldn't strike a responsive chord.

Remaining several car lengths behind Sherry's beige compact as she turned south on West Shore and drove at a decorous pace toward the city's Port Tampa section, Mike acknowledged he didn't know what to make of her. Though she was polite and seemed friendly enough, at least superficially, he continued to sense that she didn't particularly care for him. Conversely, he'd never felt such a strong attraction to anyone. Why, in face of all possible evidence to the contrary, was he willing to bet his feelings were reciprocated?

To complicate matters even further, she wasn't the sort he usually dated. Indeed, far from it. Until she'd turned up at the university that morning, he'd have said he preferred his women blond and busty, outgoing, a little frivolous. From what he knew of her, Sherry Tompkins was none of those things. Modestly endowed, with the simple, squeaky-clean coiffure of a schoolgirl, she'd blushed on blundering into his office when he was washing up. Her clear, gray eyes bespoke a seriousness of purpose he found formidable.

Yet he couldn't seem to stop watching her. Or attempting to read her thoughts. Distracted as he'd conferred with several of the coalition's board members during the break, he'd followed her progress into the kitchen with Sandy and wished he *was* the one chatting with her. Alone with her in his convertible after dropping Sandy and Hector off at their respective doorsteps, he'd fantasized about making love to her, waking up with her on a lazy Saturday, exchanging pleasantries as they nuzzled each other with their mouths.

Nobody had to tell him his thoughts were dangerous. *She's your employee, for God's sake!* he'd excoriated himself. *There's a name for what you're contemplating. You need to hang loose. Concentrate on your work. Avoid anything that even smacks of suggestive behavior where she's concerned.*

Still, as Sherry turned into her grandmother's sandspur-choked drive, got out of her car and waved him a diffident good-night, he realized that he hadn't given up hope. Bosses and their secretaries sometimes got together by mutual consent. It could happen in their case if he was patient.

Jamie was fussing as Sherry entered the house and found a replay of the scene that had greeted her that afternoon. Sound asleep and increasingly deaf in addition to her other physical ailments, Sherry's grandmother hadn't heard him whimpering. Picking him up, changing him and getting a bottle out of the refrigerator, Sherry took him out to the porch swing and did her best to rock and soothe him as he nursed. Though Jamie seemed comforted by her attentions, her own imbroglio of unsettled feelings wasn't so easy to dismiss. This miniature human being, this precious child with his tiny, perfect fingers and melting dark eyes is flesh of Mike's flesh...the product of his and Lisa's union, she thought, rubbing salt into the wound of her attraction to him. She was devastated to think that, for the second time that day, jealousy of her dead sister's relationship with Mike Ruiz had risen up to haunt her.

In the morning, both Mike and Hector were absent from FFU's storefront office on Kennedy Boulevard when Sherry reported for work. Letting herself in with the key Hector had given her, she spent most of the morning taking messages, straightening up the files and, at Hector's request, putting together a flyer that would be mailed to area churches requesting donations of money and clothing for impoverished migrants. A business major out of practicality, she'd always liked to sketch. Calling that talent into play, she embellished her creation with an original cartoon to make it more appealing and eye-catching.

A bit balky with age, the copy machine finally spit out the number of copies Sherry wanted. On her lunch break, which she took from 1:00 to 2:00 p.m., she mailed out most of them, saving a few to deliver in person to those churches she thought most likely to help. At one church in the Palma Ceia section, she found the minister in his office and willing to talk with her. Expressing an interest in her project, he promised to speak with his social-action chairman that very afternoon and get back to her.

When she finally returned to the office around 2:30 p.m., Mike was there. "Where've you been?" he asked somewhat testily. "The phone was ringing off the hook when I came in the door."

She'd forgotten to switch on the answering machine. "Sorry," she murmured, vowing not to slip up again as she handed him a sample of her work. "I was mailing . . . and, in some cases, hand delivering . . . this flyer. Hector asked me to make it. Since I did most of the necessary running around on my lunch hour, I thought it would be okay."

Gruff but secretly pleased at her initiative and the talent her cartoon betrayed, Mike followed up with a disturbing question. That morning, over coffee at a local restaurant, Hector had mentioned she had a year-old baby. Why hadn't she told *him?*

Caught off guard, Sherry was a little curt. "You didn't ask," she responded. "And I didn't think it pertinent to our discussion. If I show up for work on time, and do what's required of me, I don't see how my having a child makes any difference . . ."

It makes a difference to me, dammit, Mike thought. I want to know who his father is. Or was, if he's out of the picture. It's on the tip of my tongue to ask if you still care for him. He couldn't question her further without violating fair labor practices. And they both knew it. Smart, desirable and maddeningly distant, she had him skating on thin ice every time he took a breath.

"I was just curious about you in a friendly way," he tried to explain.

"If you don't mind, I'd like to keep my personal life personal."

Mike felt as if he'd been slapped. The fact that he probably deserved to be didn't mitigate the effect.

"Miss Tompkins, there's no need to be miffed..." he protested, a shade defensively.

They were on the verge of an actual argument when the phone shrilled. To Sherry's elation, their caller was the social-action chairman of the last church she'd visited. The woman's committee had held its regular monthly meeting that afternoon, and their minister had presented Sherry's request.

"Our members liked it," she said. "We've begun looking for an up-to-the-minute cause to support and we think this is it. We voted to hold a benefit picnic. All we need is Mike Ruiz's okay. Plus, we'd like to have him attend as guest speaker."

Her gray eyes sparkling with the first hint of enthusiasm Mike had seen in them, Sherry nodded triumphantly. "He's right here," she said with a grin. "I'll let you speak with him."

As he conversed with the committee chairman, Mike was bowled over by Sherry's success. The benefit picnic promised to bring in a wealth of badly needed contributions. Plus it might set a precedent for other churches. Their tiff over her stubborn privacy forgotten by the time he'd thanked the woman, promised to clear his calendar for her event and put down the phone, he snatched up Sherry's hand and kissed it.

"I can scarcely believe it," he exulted. "We've tried to interest that particular church in helping us for several years to no avail. Then *you* come along, and accomplish it your first full day on staff. I have to admit it...I'm impressed!"

Stunned by the spontaneous tribute, Sherry didn't acknowledge it in words. Or complain that his behavior was too familiar. I don't want to like him, she thought helplessly. Or experience the Fourth of July in my blood every time he touches me. To her distress, his touch had that precise effect. She'd just have to see to it that, for the remainder of her stint in his office, they didn't connect.

"Thanks... I appreciate the praise," she said at last, finding her voice. "If you don't mind, since I skipped eating, I'd like to run across the street for a cup of coffee and a doughnut to bring back to my desk."

Sensing her withdrawal, Mike gave his okay without missing a beat. "I'll catch the phone," he volunteered. "In my opinion, the custard-filled Berliners with chocolate frosting are the best."

The remainder of the afternoon passed almost without incident. It was only at quitting time, when they left the building simultaneously, that fate took a hand in throwing them together. Stashing his briefcase in the back of the Mustang, Mike heard Sherry's engine grind in an attempt to turn over and then give up the ghost. When she tried to resurrect it, all she got were a few sputters and gasps, followed by a series of clicks.

To Mike, it sounded like the starter. She wasn't going anywhere without assistance unless he missed his guess. "Can I do anything to help?" he asked, showing up next to the window on her driver's side.

I want to say *no*, Sherry thought. Unfortunately, if I did, I'd look like an idiot. Plus I don't fancy sitting here at the curb all night. I need to get home. Relieve Gram. And check on Jamie. "Could you possibly take a look?" she asked.

"Happy to," he answered, peeling off his suit jacket and rolling up his sleeves.

Tinkering beneath the hood of Sherry's car while she waited apprehensively, Mike quickly confirmed his off-the-cuff diagnosis. The starter would have to be replaced. He doubted she could afford it.

"Looks like the starter died," he said regretfully, emerging to meet her worried expression. "We'd better go back into the office and call a tow truck."

Sherry was stricken. "How much do starters cost?"

He shrugged, reluctant to be the bearer of bad news. "Sixty...seventy-five dollars, or so, including labor. It depends somewhat on the model."

Not responding, she hugged her arms. There wasn't a spare dime in her checking account to pay a mechanic, let alone the driver of a tow truck. She could start taking the bus to work, she supposed. But that wouldn't solve the problem of what to do with her recalcitrant vehicle. She couldn't just bury it there at the curb, could she? No doubt there was a law against it.

Sensing her despair, Mike dared to advance a proposal. "If that kind of money's a problem for you," he added gently, "maybe I could make a suggestion. I know someone who works at a garage and repairs cars on his own, in his spare time. If you want, we could call him. He has a tow bar on the back of his van and, as it happens, he owes me a favor. It might take a while for him to fix your car, but I guarantee...he'll do a good job. And he won't charge you very much."

To Sherry, Mike's advice had all the earmarks of a godsend. There was only one problem with it. Even a bargain repair job was beyond her means. Her grandmother's rent was due in a few days and they were almost out of groceries. Meanwhile, on the verge of walking, Jamie needed a sturdy pair of shoes. If only her car could have waited to break down until she'd received her first paycheck!

"That'd be terrific," she said wistfully, "if I had a little leeway in my budget. I'm, uh, financially embarrassed at the moment."

Uncertain how much help she'd accept from him, Mike decided to go for broke. "I could advance the money against your salary," he offered. "No...let me finish. With the coup you pulled off today, you deserve a bonus. At most places, you'd probably get one. Though we can't afford that, we *can* carry you a couple of weeks."

He was being so nice it made her feel guilty, despite her unflattering opinion of him. The fact is, he *owes* us, she reminded herself. If he hadn't abandoned Lisa the way he did, we wouldn't be hurting.

The rebellious mental diatribe didn't serve to blunt her gratitude the way she'd hoped. However, it did make her a little more willing to accept his assistance. "Okay...if you're serious," she agreed at last. "I promise not to make a habit of it."

Pleased she'd let him help her, Mike held open her car door for her. "C'mon," he said. "We'll phone my friend, Jerry. And then I'll drive you home."

Though he let the phone ring nearly a dozen times, Mike wasn't able to reach his mechanic pal, Jerry Suarez. They'd have to leave Sherry's car parked where it was overnight.

"Trust me...it'll be fine here," he said, ushering her into his Mustang. "This may not be the best of neighborhoods. But the folks around here look after us."

Taking him at his word, Sherry tried to relax and ignore the strong sensual awareness his close proximity seemed to evoke. As a result, she appeared preoccupied and they barely spoke during the drive south toward Port Tampa on MacDill Avenue. It was only as they approached the sagging frame house she shared with Jamie and her grandmother that he broke the silence and caused her a panicky moment.

"If you wouldn't think it pushy of me," he said, "I'd like to come in for a minute and meet your baby."

How could she refuse him, after he'd been so helpful to her? Oblivious to her hidden agenda, he'd think her mean-spirited. Yet, emotionally, she hadn't worked up to it. Attempting to count the cost, she didn't answer him for a moment. Lisa hadn't introduced Mike to their grandmother, had she? If he recognized Lillian Hayes, the jig might be up. There was a good chance he'd insist on knowing just whose baby Jamie *was*.

On a rational level, she doubted any such introduction had taken place. Painfully aware their grandmother didn't approve of her love life and straining at the bit for independence, Lisa had moved out at seventeen to share quarters with a series of roommates. She'd seldom if ever brought her boyfriends home, though she'd introduced a few of them to Sherry when they'd bumped into each other in public places.

Gram's last name is the same as Lisa's was, Sherry thought. *I'll have to avoid mentioning it if she and Mike meet, and pray she doesn't blow my cover.* The fact that Lillian Hayes didn't condone Sherry's scheme to check Mike out before demanding child support from him didn't augur well for her reticence. Still, Sherry had earned the older woman's respect by living a virtuous life, graduating from college and contributing faithfully to Jamie's support. Maybe it had been enough to win her indulgence.

She could only hope.

"It's possible Jamie'll be asleep," she said, in a half-hearted attempt to dissuade him.

Mike wasn't the type to abandon an objective once he'd fastened on it. "In that case, I'll just peek and run," he said. "I wasn't expecting a dinner invitation."

Allowing him to come in had its merits, she supposed. It would give her a chance to observe him with Jamie, and come a little closer to evaluating his fitness to be a father to the boy. So what if the tableau they made ended up tugging at her heartstrings? It was Jamie's welfare that mattered, not any selfish wish on her part to retain his exclusive custody.

"Okay," she said at last, deciding to take the risk. "I suppose I ought to warn you . . . we don't keep a very fancy household."

Mike reflected that he'd seen quite a few crummier ones as they mounted the steps to the shotgun cottage's wooden porch and entered its cramped living room. With the exception of several of Jamie's toys, which lay scattered about, the latter's overall appearance was threadbare but neat. Through an open archway, he could see and hear Sherry's grandmother, a heavyset, gray-haired woman in a faded print dress whom Hector had described to him as her grandson's baby-sitter, snoring in her overstuffed recliner on the adjacent sunporch.

"Let's not wake her if we don't have to," Sherry whispered, thankful Lillian Hayes kept her only recent photograph of Lisa on her bedroom dresser. "She hasn't been feeling particularly well the past few months."

While Mike waited for her in the living room, Sherry tiptoed out to the sunporch and held out her arms. Able to pull himself up to a standing position if he had something to hang on to, Jamie had been rocking the bars of his playpen and babbling gently to himself. Pleased to see her, he gave a delighted gurgle. Though Lillian Hayes frowned slightly at the sound, she didn't open her eyes.

Wonder of wonders, Jamie didn't need changing. Holding a finger to her lips to ensure Mike's continuing silence as she hoisted the baby onto her hip, Sherry motioned for him to follow her into the kitchen. And then felt her heart turn over as he offered Jamie a finger to grasp.

In Mike's opinion, Sherry's baby was a knockout though he didn't favor her much. "Hey, little guy...you're mighty handsome, did you know that?" he asked, grinning from ear to ear as he introduced himself. "Can you say 'hi' to your mommy's new boss? Or are you just going to hang on to her blouse and blow bubbles that way?"

"Da-da-da," Jamie answered emphatically, unaware of how devastatingly appropriate his comment was.

They were so alike, this forceful, dark-haired man with the sex appeal of a movie star and his baby son, who smiled up at him with the big, brown eyes he'd inherited. Two peas in a pod... carbon copies, really, Sherry thought, her eyes filling up with tears despite a firm resolve on her part not to let them. The acorn hadn't fallen very far from the tree in Jamie's case.

She couldn't believe Mike didn't see it instantly—any more than she could understand how a man who appeared to like children as much as he did could have turned his back on an infant he'd helped create. She had to get herself under control before she started bawling openly, and raised a billion questions. "Mind holding him a minute while I warm up his baby food and fill a bottle for him?" she asked in a shaken tone.

Mike was only too happy to comply with the request. Thoroughly smitten with his nephews and nieces, the offspring of his older brother, Joe, and Joe's wife, Kathy, he loved little kids to distraction. Whenever he had a moment to think about it, he pictured himself settling down with a wife and family of his own. He just hadn't met anyone he wanted to marry that much.

Now a slim, tawny-haired young woman with thoughts he couldn't seem to read had come into his life. And the future was anybody's guess. Meanwhile, her little boy was awfully sweet. Dandling Jamie on his knee as he relaxed in one of the spindly kitchen chairs, Mike gave the enraptured youngster a make-believe pony ride as he opened his mind to a host of possibilities.

Busy heating Jamie's dinner in a pan of water on the stove, and then removing him from Mike's lap so she could place him in his high chair, Sherry tried not to glance at Mike too much. I have to be hardheaded about this, she thought. Decide what's best for Jamie in a practical vein. I can't let myself be swept away on a torrent of emotion.

Watching her loving concentration as she fed the baby, Mike had a better opportunity to observe the boy. Once again, he began to speculate about the man who'd fathered him. A question arose in his mind and then got put on hold as, mopping the remains of Jamie's pureed chicken and chunky applesauce from his chin with one corner of his terry cloth bib, Sherry suggested they give him his bottle on the front porch swing.

"It'll be too hot to sit outdoors when summer rolls around," she explained. "We might as well take advantage of the cooler weather."

Was it possible she was warming to him a little?

"Sounds good to me," he said.

About to congratulate herself on getting Mike out of the house before a meeting could take place, Sherry winced as they crossed the living room. A passing ambulance had awakened her grandmother.

"Sherry?" the older woman called in a querulous voice.

"Right here, Gram," Sherry replied. "I'm on my way out to the porch, to give Jamie his bottle."

"Who's that with you?"

There wasn't any help for it. She'd have to introduce them. Indicating that Mike should follow her, she led him onto the sunporch. "Gram, this is Mike Ruiz, my new boss," she said, hoping the situation wouldn't blow up in her face. "Mr. Ruiz, I'd like you to meet my grandmother."

If Mike was aware that she'd omitted her grandmother's name, he gave no sign of it. "How do you do, ma'am?" he said, offering his hand.

For a moment, Sherry thought her grandmother might refuse to take it. She let out a sigh of relief when, after putting on her glasses and squinting up at him in keen appraisal, Lillian Hayes finally did.

She might have known the older woman wouldn't let her off the hook that easily. "Now that I know who you are, what are you doing here?" she asked their dark-haired visitor.

The remark would have been rude coming from anyone but the very young or the very old. Mike considered it in that light and decided not to take offense. Glancing at Sherry and noting her discomfort, he concluded reluctantly that maybe he'd better go. She and her grandmother appeared to be at odds over something.

"Your granddaughter's car broke down and I drove her home," he answered with due respect. "It's been nice meeting you, ma'am. See you tomorrow, Miss Tompkins. Since I plan to arrive at the office around 9:00 a.m., it wouldn't be any problem to pick you up."

Her cheeks flushed with embarrassment, Sherry murmured that she'd take the bus.

Thanking Mike again at the door, she returned with Jamie to the sunporch and settled into an armchair beside her grandmother's recliner to give him his bottle. Neither woman spoke for a moment.

It wasn't long before Lillian Hayes voiced her opinion, as Sherry had known she would. It wasn't good. But then, she hadn't expected it to be.

"So that's Mike Ruiz...the man that done my Lisa wrong," Sherry's grandmother grumbled, pronouncing his name as if she'd just taken some bitter-tasting medicine. "If you'll listen to me, gal, you won't have nothin' further to do with him. We don't need his charity. Messin' around with him will only bring you grief. Don't say I didn't warn you."

Chapter Three

When Sherry arrived at FFU headquarters the following morning after a seemingly interminable bus ride from her grandmother's house, Mike was already there, conferring with several of his board members in his private office. Catching sight of her through its open doorway, he smiled and motioned for her to join the group gathered around his desk.

"Grab a notebook," he requested.

Having spent most of the previous evening mentally comparing the lively glint in his dark eyes with that of his baby son's and meditating on the poignant irony that Mike could hold Jamie on his knee without guessing their relationship, she was keenly attuned to the smallest nuances of his behavior. His friendly demeanor and lack of formality confirmed her suspicion that they'd crossed a Rubicon of sorts. Allowing him to come in, see Jamie and meet her grandmother had cast her project to check him out in a new light. Henceforth, she'd conduct it at close quarters and suffer the emotional consequences.

As she quickly found out, the unscheduled meeting in Mike's office had been called to discuss his decision to picket a citrus-processing plant in Lakeland the following afternoon. The plant in question regularly accepted fruit from several midsize growers known for their unfair labor practices and shabby treatment of itinerant laborers. Mike had prevailed on the plant's management several times to ban the growers' produce as an inducement to clean up their act—without success. Now he wanted to demonstrate. Before setting out with placards and an armload of flyers urging the plant's employees to strike in support of the pickers, he'd alert the media. He hoped a reporter for one of the local papers or TV stations would investigate.

"You know what the setup's like at Brabant-Myer," a gray-haired man with glasses warned. "The employee parking lot's inside the fence. You'll hafta trespass on private property to hand out flyers to the workers. They ain't gonna stop and take them from you as they drive out the gate."

"Oscar's right," a heavy-set woman who frequently spoke before the Hillsborough County Commission chimed in. "You'll be arrested...mark my words."

Mike shrugged, clearly aware of the possibility. "If I am, it won't be the first time," he said.

Eyes lowered as her pen flew across the pages of her stenographer's notebook, Sherry thought how difficult it would be to love a man like him, even if it weren't for his hit-and-run attitude where women were concerned. Anyone who cared for him would be worried sick over the way he thrust himself into difficult and dangerous situations.

His sangfroid didn't cause the gray-haired man to lose his frowning skepticism. "Who's going with you?" he prodded. "The usual suspects?"

It was a short list. "Hector. Frank Suarez, Jerry's brother. Maybe Sandra, if she can get off work." Mike paused. "As always, we'll keep Sandra out of harm's way...off the plant grounds, in this case. If they call the police, and we get taken into custody, she can post our bail.''

A small silence ensued in which Mike's board members appeared to give the matter further thought. Abruptly, the gray-haired man dropped his objections. Perhaps he'd intended to do so all along. ''So...'' he said gruffly, but with an unmistakable hint of admiration in his voice. ''Do what you think best, Miguelito. You will anyway.''

His fellow board members, each of whom clearly liked and approved of Mike as much as he did, quickly followed his lead.

Shaking hands and thanking each of them for coming as they filed out of his office, Mike detained Sherry for a moment. ''How's your grandmother today?'' he asked with what appeared to be genuine concern, lightly resting a tanned, beautifully shaped hand on her forearm. ''A bit more up to caring for your little guy, I hope.''

She could have protested the familiarity—raised Cain with him over it. But she didn't. Despite the sheen of gooseflesh that spread up her arms and a corresponding leap of imagination that brought a flush to her cheeks, she didn't consider it deliberately provocative. She'd seen for herself that Mike Ruiz was the kind of man who touched people when he was talking to them. Besides, she was too overwhelmed by the flood of guilt and self-pity his words had evoked to object.

Much as it pained her to admit the truth, she couldn't argue that Lillian Hayes was an appropriate caregiver for Jamie. Plainly, the older woman hadn't been able to devote the requisite energy to the task the previous afternoon. And Mike had noticed. Yet Sherry couldn't afford to hire anyone to take her place. How was she supposed to correct the situation?

The problem had left her feeling very isolated. Since Jamie's birth and Lisa's death two months later, no one had commiserated over the heavy burden of responsibility that had been shifted to her shoulders. It had simply been assumed she would carry it. No one had voiced the slightest sympathy over the worries it had entailed.

That the first measure of compassion over the difficulties she faced should come from Mike was ironic, to say the least. If he'd lived up to his responsibilities, she wouldn't *be* in the difficulty she was in. Paradoxically, she yearned to lean on him—rest her head on his shoulder and weep until her tears had soaked completely through his shirt.

"Actually," she admitted, hanging on to the shreds of her dignity as if clutching them with her fingernails, "Gram's about the same. I know she shouldn't fall asleep when she's watching Jamie . . . that it could actually be dangerous. I'm well aware she won't be able to care for him much longer in any event, now that he's on the verge of walking. Yet I can't afford to pay a sitter. Or put him in day care. I don't know what . . . I'm going to do. . . ."

His heart going out to her, Mike wondered where her baby's father was. Why hadn't he offered to do his part? Or been forced to help her legally? No pushover, from what he'd been able to determine, Sherry must have a fairly powerful reason for going it alone, he thought.

He gave her arm a little squeeze. "Let's take the matter under advisement," he suggested. "Though it's been less than a week since you started here, you're a valued employee. If we put our heads together, maybe we can come up with a solution that will make your life a little easier."

The exquisite incongruity of his comments almost too much for her to bear, Sherry bit her lip. A short time later, without her having to lift a finger to make it happen, her car was towed away by Mike's mechanic friend, Jerry Suarez, as she watched through FFU's plate glass window.

"Did he say anything about what the repairs will cost?" she asked Mike worriedly from his office doorway.

Glancing up from his desk, he gave her a satisfied grin. "Jerry agreed to do the work for $20 plus some scrap lumber I have stored at my father's house," he said. "If that's a strain on your budget, you can pay me back in installments."

Hastily calculating how to squeeze that sum from her weekly grocery bill, Sherry informed him that $20 was manageable. "As for the lumber..." she began.

With obvious reluctance, Mike admitted the boards in question weren't really scrap, but rather a stack of perfectly good two-by-fours a private client had given him in lieu of payment.

Incredibly, the man who'd broken Lisa's heart and left her to bear their child alone was like some country doctor, willing to accept in-kind recompense for some pills or a house call.

"I can't let you pay my debts for me," she protested.

He dismissed the objection with a casual wave. "Only temporarily," he insisted. "Besides... Jerry's building a playhouse for his kid. And my dad's been nagging me to get rid of that lumber for some time. Everybody benefits."

Her emotions even more hopelessly tangled than before, Sherry retreated to her desk. Contrary to expectation, Mike was *nice* as well as sexy. Or at least, that was how it seemed. He appeared ready and willing to pull what strings he could for anyone in trouble. With his farmworkers' union, he'd turned the frequently lucrative practice of law into a helping profession.

Yet conversely he'd abandoned her sister and turned his back on their little boy. She had every reason to hate him. Somehow she had to regard him as an adversary.

The following morning, she reached the office before he did. His private line was ringing as she unlocked the door. "Good morning, Florida Farmworkers' Union," she said breathlessly, picking up the phone.

"Hi, Sherry." Like her brother's, Sandra Ruiz's voice was warm and friendly as it came over the line. "I've got bad news, I'm afraid," she said. "Mike wanted me to join on his Lakeland picket this afternoon, and I won't be able to. A major spouse abuse case just came in. Tell him for me that I'm really sorry, okay?"

"Will do," Sherry replied, wondering who'd bail Mike and his friends out, if necessary, in his sister's absence.

"I don't suppose . . . *you'd* be willing to do it," Sandra speculated, as if she'd read Sherry's thoughts.

Murmuring something about her need to remain in the office, Sherry didn't make any promises. Yet, as she replaced the receiver, her thoughts were racing. I want to go, she admitted. Not because I want to help him out, or hang out with him. But because it's a worthy cause. And I want to see him under stress. That's the best time to evaluate anyone.

She was subdued when Mike walked in—the perfect secretary, doing her job with a minimum of fuss. Relaying Sandra's message and noting that he appeared thoroughly inconvenienced by it, she added offhandedly, "If you want, I could go in her place."

"You, Sherry?"

The idea had taken him by surprise. Focusing his expressive, dark eyes on her with the intensity of a laser, he probed her motivation. In the short time she'd worked for him, he'd felt the barriers go up each time he'd so much as considered the possibility they might be more to each other than employer and employee someday. That had been particularly true the night he'd taken her home, asked to come in and met her grandmother. She'd been nervous as a cat, keeping him at arm's length. Though he continued to feel sparks fly between them, and he was willing to bet she felt them, too, he'd concluded she wanted nothing to do with him.

Now she was volunteering to help, actively courting a situation in which they'd be thrown together. What was going on?

She didn't flinch at the scrutiny. "Why not?" she insisted. "Give me one good reason. The fact is, you need my help."

Mike's mouth softened despite his reservations. "One good reason, you say? Well, what about *Jamie?* There are likely to be some arrests this afternoon. We can't have him pining away while his mommy languishes in the hoosegow."

Her mind made up, Sherry wasn't about to be deterred so easily. Even Mike's blatant sexiness—his dangerous but appealing wild animal quality—didn't spur her to caution. It only added to her exhilarating sense of parachuting behind enemy lines, accepting a hazardous assignment. So what if he thinks I'm chasing him? she thought. It's for a reason. I'll be setting him straight soon enough.

"I took notes at yesterday's meeting, remember?" she reminded him. "Sandra was supposed to stay on public property, bail you out if necessary. I don't see how that could be so dangerous."

She had him there. Besides, he wanted her with him, when it came right down to it. She might not be his type, this sleek, standoffish, exceedingly proper young woman. But he had a thing for her. There wasn't any use denying it. Knowing she'd be on hand to back him up gave him a warm and tender feeling deep in his gut.

"Okay, if you're serious," he acquiesced. "We'll be leaving for Lakeland around 2:00 p.m. Hector and Frank Suarez, the brother of the man who's fixing your car, will meet us there. I'll drive you past the bail bondsman's place first, so you'll know where it is if you have to deal with him."

Instead of asking her to do it for him, as his secretary, Mike called the newspapers and TV stations himself. Perhaps that was because he knew most of the reporters he was trying to reach on a first name basis. From her desk, Sherry could hear him laughing and exchanging tart remarks with one of them. Mary Murchison, she surmised with distaste. The blonde from Channel 11. *The way she hangs on him, they've probably been to bed together.* There wasn't much doubt in her mind that they'd see Mary and her camera crew at the plant site if Mike suggested it.

The fact that Mary Murchison looked a lot like Lisa, though she had considerably more class and self-confidence, didn't make Sherry feel any better. Neither did the jealousy of her dead sister's relationship with Mike that she couldn't seem to quell. She felt as if she were selling her sister short with one hand, and coveting what little happiness Lisa had known with the other. As a result, she was guilt-ridden and thoroughly unhappy with herself when, following her lunch hour, she got into Mike's Mustang with him for the trip to Lakeland.

If only my negative feelings about him would prevent me from noticing the bewitching little muscle that quirks beside his mouth, she thought. *Or imagining his lips on mine.* Unfortunately, her mind didn't seem to work that way. For better or worse, Mike Ruiz had the kind of presence a woman encountered just once or twice in a lifetime. Or so she guessed. He might be selfish, irresponsible, even heartless, as Lisa had claimed. But those qualities didn't stand out at first blush. What she'd seen to date was a warmhearted guy who stood ready to help anyone in trouble—one whose impassioned lovemaking, she suspected, could send her soaring outside herself.

Already humid and overcast, the day turned rainy as they drove past the office of Mike's preferred bail bondsman in Lakeland and joined forces with Frank and Hector outside the citrus-processing plant they planned to picket. On the trip over, Mike had worried aloud that one or more members of the press might have contacted the plant manager for a comment, causing the gates to be shut in advance of their arrival. To his relief, that hadn't happened. They'd be able to waltz right through.

"Stay here," he ordered, indicating that Sherry should remain beside the Mustang, which was parked on the public right-of-way. "If we get arrested, I want you to go straight to the bail bondsman's office and give him the money in this envelope. He'll know what to do. Don't set foot in the plant parking lot under any circumstances."

Gazing soberly up at him, Sherry murmured a hesitant, "Okay."

What did she think was going to happen? That the plant manager would unleash guard dogs on them? "Don't panic... everything's going to be fine," he assured her, absurdly gratified that she'd worry about him.

It was 2:53 p.m. By now, employees who worked the afternoon shift were arriving in a steady stream. The much larger day shift would come pouring out at any moment.

Nodding, Sherry leaned against the Mustang's rear fender and watched as Mike's protest unfolded. To her surprise, he and his companions entered the parking lot unchallenged. They were able to position themselves directly outside the factory entrance. While Frank held up a placard denouncing the plant's policy of accepting fruit from growers who mistreated their pickers, Mike and Hector began handing out the stack of flyers urging labor solidarity that Sherry had designed and reproduced for them.

Though they looked somewhat askance at the trio of demonstrators, many of the arriving employees accepted flyers. So did a number of their departing co-workers. A management representative and the Channel 11 news team, with Mary Murchison in the lead, arrived on the scene within seconds of each other—just in time for the latter to videotape the former as he ordered Mike and company off the grounds.

Predictably, they didn't budge. The head-to-head confrontation that followed, marked by tightly controlled anger on the plant representative's part and reasonable stubbornness on Mike's, would enliven the six o'clock news, Sherry guessed.

Another TV crew and several print reporters had materialized by the time the plant representative retreated into the building, in all likelihood to phone the authorities. Seemingly unruffled by the probable outcome of their intransigence, Hector and Frank went on attempting to hand out flyers while Mike took time out to answer reporters' questions. Now comes the arrest part, Sherry thought, a little lump of tension forming in the pit of her stomach. Mike's made his point and the press has duly noted it. Why doesn't he beat a graceful retreat before the police arrive?

But she knew the answer as well as he did. If he surrendered without a fight, his protest would lose all sense of urgency. The priority rating of the resulting news coverage would slip. He'd have failed to achieve the only goal within his reach. Handcuffed by police, he became a martyr. The media would gobble up a dramatic event with a touch of heroism for their audience.

It wasn't long before sirens were wailing in the distance, headed in their direction. They'd attained an ear-splitting level by the time two Polk County Sheriff's squad cars rolled into the processing-plant compound.

As Sherry watched from the sidelines, the plant representative reappeared with several minions at his heels. After listening to his complaint, one of the sheriff's deputies addressed Mike. He pointed to a No Tresspassing sign. Attempting to argue earned Mike a pair of handcuffs. Their materials confiscated and stuffed in a trash bin, Hector and Frank Suarez were similarly manacled. Clearly confident that officers would back him up, the plant representative ordered the press off the premises.

With a photographer from the Lakeland *Ledger* snapping away and TV cameras rolling as the cameramen operating them backed slowly toward the exit, the three men were escorted to waiting squad cars. Sherry caught a glimpse of Mike's face as they were driven through the gate. She thought he seemed more satisfied than upset, as if he'd gotten exactly what he wanted.

Sliding behind the Mustang's steering wheel and inserting Mike's key in the ignition, she sat quietly for a moment, attempting to regain her perspective. I'm in the driver's seat...literally, she thought. If I don't bail Mike out, he's going to spend some time behind bars. In my book, he deserves it for the way he treated my nephew and my sister.

The part of her that didn't want to believe in his culpability objected. If you hope to get his cooperation with Jamie, it argued, you can't afford to abandon him that way. She refused to acknowledge that seeing handcuffs slapped on his wrists had touched her in a vulnerable place.

The bail bondsman's office was empty of other customers when Sherry arrived. "Mike Ruiz and a couple of his buddies?" the freckled, overweight owner grinned in response to her tentative question. "Sure thing, honey. I'll call over to the county jail...see if their bond's been set."

Digging the money Mike had given her out of her purse as the bail bondsman mumbled something into the telephone, Sherry was astonished to learn it wouldn't be needed. "Your boyfriend and his pals are gonna be released," he said, his grin widening as he hung up. "They should be ready to go by the time you get over there."

The man's casual assumption that Mike was her boyfriend, compounded by her own monumental relief that his arrest had been rescinded, prompted Sherry to think some uneasy thoughts as she drove the short distance to the county jail. No way are you going to let yourself care for him, she chastised herself as she parked and waited. Where

Lisa and Jamie are concerned, that would be the ultimate insult.

Despite her vow, she felt the tension in her stomach un-coil as—following a forty-five-minute wait that had caused her to imagine all sorts of things—Mike finally appeared, followed by Hector and Frank Suarez. His demeanor was lighthearted, triumphant as he motioned for her to move over so he could get behind the wheel.

"The plant manager wised up and decided not to press charges," he explained as his companions got in behind them. "Unfortunately for him, he did it a little late. We get the credit—and the publicity—for going to jail, whereas he looks uncaring, indecisive and guilty by association."

They'd miss the local news if they drove straight back to Tampa without stopping on the way. And Mike wanted to assess their coverage. "Mind dropping by a tavern I know and watching a little television?" he asked Sherry as they slowed to a stop beside Frank's truck. "You can phone your grandmother when we get there...make sure she's on the job. The overtime you earn will help pay for your car repairs."

Like him, Sherry was curious about the news coverage that would result from their efforts. Plus she could cer-tainly use the extra cash. "I suppose that'd be all right," she answered, telling herself the reasons she'd cited were her only ones.

In response, Mike patted her hand, sending the by-now expected wave of gooseflesh skidding up her arm. "Hec-tor, Frank...meet us at Flanagan's, okay?" he said. "We'll see you there."

At Flanagan's, a roadhouse situated on the outskirts of nearby Plant City which featured country music on the jukebox and an ersatz cowboy decor, Mike ordered beers for everyone. Seated with her three male companions at the bar, Sherry was keenly aware of the regulars' stares and the way Mike's knee kept accidentally brushing hers.

She forgot the former, though not the latter, as WTPA's six o'clock news flashed on the overhead television screen. To everyone's delight, Mike's picketing story was the second lead. Voiced in response to Mary Murchison's questions, his plea for an industry boycott of those growers who treated their migrant laborers poorly was allowed to remain unchallenged.

"After phoning Polk County sheriff's deputies to ask that the demonstrators be forcibly removed from its employee parking lot, Brabant-Myer abruptly dropped its complaint," the attractive blond newswoman reported as she posed with her Channel 11 microphone outside the chain-link fence that encircled the plant compound. "When asked whether his firm planned to stop accepting fruit from the growers in question, a company spokesman declined comment."

Clicking his glass against those of his companions, Mike proposed a toast. "To our success this afternoon!" he declared. "And to better treatment for migrants. Maybe we should go for a consumer boycott. Or, maybe..."

His euphoria fading into contemplation, he gazed at a poster announcing a pocket billiards tournament without really seeing it. "What are you thinking, Miguelito?" Hector asked.

As Sherry watched, the dark-haired man who'd begun to consume most of her waking thoughts despite her disparaging opinion of him gave his characteristic shrug. "Just that we ought to go undercover at one of the holdout camps," he mused. "Highlight the abuses that are happening there. Maybe then we'd provoke some real change, not just a few lukewarm statements of outrage that barely create a blip on the public consciousness."

Aware he could get beaten up and dumped in a ditch, or handed a prison sentence for what he was proposing, Sherry forgot her carefully contrived position of neutrality. "You can't be serious!" she protested.

Hector and Frank exchanged a look.

"Ah, but I am," Mike said. "If you want to serve justice, you have to take some risks."

On that pensive note, their celebration broke up. Anxious to leave because he was scheduled to teach a night class at Hillsborough Community College, Frank Suarez volunteered to drop off Hector. As before, Sherry would ride with Mike. He'd take her straight to her grandmother's house. By now, it was fully dark and he wouldn't hear of letting her take the bus from the office.

They didn't talk much on the way. It was only when Mike pulled to the curb outside Lillian Hayes' raised frame cottage that she learned what kind of ideas he'd been turning over in his head.

"Sherry," he murmured, detaining her with the volatile medium of his touch, "we need to talk."

What about? she thought with an explosive little shudder. Surely you haven't guessed my purpose! "Can't it wait until tomorrow?" she asked, reaching for the door handle. "It's getting late. And I want to check on Jamie..."

"This is *about* Jamie." Mike's gaze compelled her to hear him out as he fixed it on her in the shadowy convertible. "I've been thinking about him. Your need to work. And your worries that your grandmother isn't up to caring for him. What about his father? Doesn't he provide child support?" Stricken, Sherry ducked the question. "That's none of your business!" she exclaimed.

His answer was calm, supportive, nonthreatening. "Maybe not," he admitted. "I won't argue the point. I'd just like to say I care, and that I know someone who might be able to watch your baby for you. Her name is Marta Ramirez and she runs a day care center a few blocks from our office. We've been friends for years and, when I explained your situation to her, she agreed to give you a special rate."

Furious he'd gossip about her with a stranger, and horrified to be discussed as a charity case, Sherry didn't bother to soften her inflection. The words came out of her mouth as rough as sandpaper.

"What did you say to make her do that?"

"Just that you're a valued employee. And...I hope...a friend..."

Seconds later, the unthinkable was happening. There in the dim, cramped confines of his convertible while her grandmother and Jamie waited for her inside the house, the man Lisa had accused of betrayal was lowering his lips to hers. With a sigh of regret and helplessness that hinted he, too, had reservations about getting involved, he was parting them, so that they seemed to breathe the same breath.

Trapped in a vortex of conflicting emotions, Sherry couldn't seem to move or speak. Never had a man made her feel so completely alive, yet so defenseless, as if she shook on the brink of some staggering discovery. Never had one so effortlessly pushed past the limits she'd set for herself.

Conversely, she'd never disliked—or distrusted—a man so much. No! the righteous avenger in her screamed. You can't do this. Not with Lisa's lover. It isn't right!

To her consternation, the primitive inner woman who sat in judgment of such things didn't object. Melting, softening, blurring into the heat of their connection, *that* woman was kissing the Mike Ruiz she knew, not some ogre from one of Lisa's fairy tales. With delight, she was celebrating an onslaught of feeling that penetrated to the soles of her feet, exulting in her unexpected emergence from what she'd feared would turn out to be a permanent desert of the heart.

Chapter Four

Another moment, and she'd be lost. Like her sister before her, she'd surrender her heart to a man who loved women easily but not well. Too principled to go to bed with him and end up pregnant the way Lisa had, she'd be injured in a less obvious sense. Already wary of men, thanks to the track record several generations of women in her family had chalked up with them, she'd isolate herself even further. Her dream of finding Mr. Right and settling down with him to raise a family might be permanently crushed.

She'd also be complicating her project—maybe to the point of rendering it totally ineffective. Gulping, she found her voice. "Mike, please ... we can't do this!" she protested.

Contrary to her expectation, he desisted at once. "Why not?" he asked reasonably, his mouth still tantalizingly close. "Because I'm your boss and you're my employee? If it's what we both want ..."

Her strength to oppose him returning, Sherry reached for the door handle. "As far as I'm concerned, it isn't," she replied, hoping she spoke the truth as she got out and addressed him from the curb. "Friendship's okay, since we have to work together. But that's absolutely *all* I'm willing to accept."

For once Lillian Hayes was awake when Sherry walked into the house. Gazing at her granddaughter's face, she slowly shook her head. "Not you too, gal."

Though Sherry's demeanor remained steadfast, she couldn't keep her cheeks from reddening. "I'd burn in hell first," she attested.

Busy with Jamie, she let the older woman get the phone when it rang some twenty minutes later. "Sher...it's for you," Lillian Hayes called out from the sunporch, her tone fraught with disapproval. "I think it's your boss."

With great reluctance, Sherry hoisted Jamie onto her hip and emerged from the kitchen to accept the receiver. Her caller was Mike, as her grandmother had guessed. Whatever else had occurred, it seemed, they'd progressed to a first name basis.

"Before you say anything, Sherry," he told her without preamble, "I'd like to apologize for misreading you a few minutes ago. We've only known each other a short time, yet I value your friendship. If that's all you want from me...in addition to your weekly paycheck, of course...then that's all you'll get."

She didn't answer, prompting him to add, "I promise. No more shenanigans. Understood?"

It was time for her to say something. "Yes, all right," she answered, wondering why she should feel such an overpowering sense of loss.

"Good. That's settled, then." Mike's husky baritone took on a persuasive note. "About my friend's day care center—"

"I thought I told you—"

"That's true...you did. But you didn't let me finish. The fact is, Marta owes me a favor. And helping you fits that category. From a purely selfish standpoint, I don't want your child care problems to affect your work.''

Involuntarily, she glanced at her grandmother. Keenly focused on her at the beginning of their conversation, the older woman's attention had strayed to the television set. Though Jamie had begun fussing and wriggling to be free of Sherry's grasp, she didn't offer to take the baby. Or even glance in their direction. Her face puffier and more spent-looking than Sherry had ever seen it, she stared fixedly at a game show that probably didn't even interest her.

Watching an eleven-month-old child is too much for Gram, Sherry thought. I ought to accept, if only for her sake. The same kind of reasoning applied to Jamie. Despite both their efforts, Lisa's precious little boy wasn't getting the care he deserved. Meanwhile, Mike owed them. It was only right he should do his part.

"When you put it like that, I suppose I ought to look into your suggestion," she said finally. "How do I go about doing that?"

Clearly pleased she'd consider letting him help her, Mike gave her Marta Ramirez's address and phone number. It seemed she cared for her young charges in a partially renovated Hyde Park bungalow that also served as her residence. "Why not stop by tomorrow on your way to work and talk with her?" he suggested. "Things can be a bit hectic at that hour, with kids getting dropped off right and left. But it would be a good time to judge her competence."

His kiss still wreaking havoc with her peace of mind and lighting a bonfire in her imagination, Sherry was eager to end their conversation as quickly as possible. She wanted to do what needed to be done for Jamie and grab a moment alone. Chatting with Mike on the phone as if nothing had happened only made the situation seem more incongruous.

"I will. Thanks for thinking of me," she said a bit stiffly, hoping he could take a hint.

He could. And did. "Don't mention it," he answered in a correspondingly businesslike tone. "Have a good night's rest."

As Sherry put down the phone and shifted Jamie to her other hip, a thought that had hovered at the threshold of her consciousness abruptly clarified. To her knowledge, other than Jamie, whom he hadn't acknowledged as his, Mike didn't have a small child to drop off for Marta Ramirez's supervision. Yet he'd described the early morning scene at her combined residence and day care center with offhand familiarity. What had he been doing there at that hour? Soliciting her help with some project? Or adjusting his tie and drinking a farewell cup of coffee after spending the night in her bed? If Marta Ramirez was young and sexy, it had been the latter, Sherry guessed.

Overflowing with misgivings and unanswered questions when she arrived at the Sunshine Day Care Center on Howard Avenue the following morning, Sherry got a warm welcome from its slim, thirty-something director.

"Any friend of Mike's is a friend of mine," Marta Ramirez said with a smile as she shook hands and then bent to wipe a toddler's runny nose. "Come in . . . sit down if you can find a place. For you, the fee will be $35 a week. Ask me whatever you want."

Attired in tennis shoes, form-fitting leggings and a voluminous sweatshirt that failed to hide her stunning figure, the day care provider had a natural panache and inborn elegance Sherry guessed would be very attractive to the opposite sex. All too easily, she could picture Mike romancing her, Marta nestling in his embrace.

A moment later she was reading herself the riot act for giving a damn about his escapades, and training her attention on the center's operation. She had to admit Marta's forthright answers to her questions—along with the woman's warm-hearted but efficient handling of her small charges—laid to rest any qualms she might have had on Jamie's behalf.

She couldn't argue about the fee. It was ridiculously low for a usually expensive service. It'll be tough to come up with the extra money, Sherry thought. Yet maybe it can be arranged. I still have Mama's aquamarine brooch. And the pearl necklace Gram gave me at my high school graduation. They might bring enough at a pawnbroker's shop to see us through until Mike starts contributing to his son's support.

To her self-disgust, she still wanted to know if Mike and Marta were—or had been—lovers. It's within my purview if I'm to weigh his fitness as a parent, she rationalized. After the way he treated Lisa, I'll need to assess his dealings with women in general, take any promiscuity into account. I don't want Jamie growing up with warped values. Or seeing things he shouldn't if visitation is arranged.

"Have you known Mike long?" she asked, precipitously changing the subject.

Marta shot her a look. "Three years," she answered without hesitation. "He defended my father in a lawsuit. Why do you ask?"

"I was wondering why you'd agree to take my son at a reduced rate."

"I see." Her hands free for the moment, the other woman strode to her kitchen counter and poured out two mugs of darkly aromatic Cuban coffee. Glancing at Sherry, she raised an inquiring eyebrow.

"Black, please," Sherry supplied.

Adding a hearty dose of sugar and cream to her own cup, Marta took a sip before answering Sherry's initial question. "I thought Mike explained," she murmured at last. "I owe him a favor. He defended my father free of charge.

But that's not what you're asking, is it? You want to know about our personal relationship."

Sherry vehemently shook her head, denying what was clearly the case. "That's none of my business," she protested.

"You're right," Marta agreed. "It isn't. But I don't mind telling you. Mike and I used to be involved. I still think highly of him . . . catch up on his life whenever I get a chance."

Stone-faced, Sherry didn't comment as she waited for the other shoe to drop.

"I won't ask if he's shown an interest in you," Marta added. "Or if you're smitten with him. You wouldn't be human if he didn't make you feel *something*. For what it's worth, he's a terrific guy . . . kind to children, animals and people in trouble. Unfortunately, from the perspective of a woman who wants a life with someone, he isn't husband material."

As she left the day care center after arranging to bring Jamie there in the morning, Sherry was confused and upset. Her negative feelings only seemed to intensify when she reached the office and learned that Mike had left for Tallahassee to lobby a select group of state legislators. A bill he supported that would set higher minimum-pay standards and mandate improved working conditions for migrant laborers had unexpectedly hit a snag in committee. He'd be gone for the better part of the week, according to Hector's best estimate.

My car isn't fixed, and now Mike won't be here to prod Jerry Suarez into completing the job, she thought irritably. Plus I won't be able to finish my evaluation of him. I was hoping I could do that—and confront him about his duty to Jamie, if that seems feasible—by the end of the second week. She spent her time answering the phone, registering several complaints from migrants, designing a flyer for Hector and typing some fairly boring letters Mike had left for her, telling herself those inconveniences were at the root of her uneasiness.

That evening, after Jamie was tucked into his crib, Sherry prowled so restlessly around her grandmother's modest dwelling that the older woman finally begged her to "light someplace."

Given the mood she was in, watching television wouldn't do the trick. Neither would sitting outside on the porch swing and counting stars. Before long, she'd be pumping the swing so violently that it would bang against the house.

"Mind if I get out some of the old pictures?" she asked with sudden inspiration, recalling a conversation she'd had with Lisa shortly before her sister's death.

Lillian Hayes gave a disinterested shrug. "Be my guest. Just put 'em back where you found 'em."

Retrieving the cardboard shoe box of loose photos she was looking for from her grandmother's bedroom closet, Sherry carried it into her own, much smaller room and emptied it on the bed. Yes, *there* was the snapshot she wanted...one she'd seen for the first time when Lisa had shown it to her during the early days of her romance with Mike Ruiz.

In it, Lisa and Mike had been standing with their backs to the rail of a cruise ship that made daily trips into the Gulf of Mexico so that its passengers could gamble beyond the twelve-mile limit. The day had been breezy and her sister's carefully permed and tinted blond hair had blown partway across her face. Yet her happiness, as she'd snuggled in the curve of Mike's arm, had lit up the photographer's lens.

Jamie's parents before his conception, Sherry thought, a lump forming in her throat. Mike looks so handsome and loving and protective. How could he have abandoned her when he knew she was carrying his baby?

That an abandonment of that sort had occurred, she had little doubt. Given her sister's record with men, she'd been skeptical at first—sufficiently dubious to confront Lisa on the subject a week before her death.

Their conversation had taken place on the porch one afternoon when Sherry was home from Gainesville for a three-day weekend. She'd been snapping pole beans preparatory to cooking them for dinner. Lounging beside her on the swing in a faded print wrapper while Jamie slept in his bassinet at her feet, Lisa had contemplated what she labeled "the ruins" of her previously spectacular figure.

"Mike Ruiz did me in pretty good," she'd complained with a rueful twist of her mouth, clearly expecting her younger sister to sympathize. "Just look at me! This nursing business has turned my breasts into udders. My stomach still bulges as if I were pregnant. Besides, even if I could manage to get back in shape, it's hopeless. What man would want me when he found out I was dragging around some other guy's baby?"

Convinced her new little nephew was the most miraculous being she'd ever set eyes upon, Sherry had strenuously objected. "You can't be serious, Lisa!" she'd cried. "Don't you *love* Jamie?"

Challenged, her sister had erupted in her face. "Of course I do, you dumb little twit. It's just that I don't know how I'm going to manage..."

Unable to fathom how a man could turn his back on his own child, Sherry had been fretting over that very question. Emboldened despite her sister's shrewish mood by their unusually frank discussion, she'd picked that moment to state it. "Are you sure Mike Ruiz *knows* about the baby?" she asked with a frown. "That you've actually told him, sis?"

Initially faltering at the straightforward demand for information, Lisa had quickly recovered. "What do you take me for...a nut case?" she'd exclaimed. "Not only does Mike know, he's refused me any hope of child support."

Somehow, Sherry had summoned the fortitude to persist. "On what grounds?" she'd asked. "Surely a judge..."

Her sister's face had crumpled in self-pity at her words, becoming a travesty of its former self. "You'll want to slap him when you hear," she'd stated. "He claims he was just one among many who shacked up with me during the relevant time period."

Expected to exclaim in horror, Sherry hadn't. Instead, hating herself but knowing Lisa all too well, she'd demanded to know whether there was any truth to Mike Ruiz's accusation.

Seated now on her bed, she remembered the look of actual fear that had come over her sister's face.

"It was a filthy lie!" Glancing hastily over her shoulder to make sure their grandmother wasn't listening, Lisa had whispered the words in a kind of muted shriek. "I may have run around a lot before meeting Mike," she'd admitted more softly. "But that was over, I swear. The truth is, I'd fallen for him. If you don't believe me, take a look at Jamie. They have the same coloring."

Shaking her head over the layers of emotion that had begun to color and distort her feelings about Mike Ruiz since going to work for him, Sherry vowed to discard them like unwanted baggage. Come what might, she'd be true to the promise she'd made herself a dozen days after the conversation on the porch swing—at her sister's funeral.

She'd believe Lisa, despite the still, small voice deep in her gut that continued to express doubt, and to hint Lisa might have been lying at some level. More importantly, she'd finish what she'd set out to do. She'd come to a decision about Mike's fitness as a parent without any more "shenanigans," as he'd put it. If he proved suitable, she'd demand child support from him, even fight him for it, if necessary. To date, she'd shown a disturbing readiness to follow in Lisa's footsteps. Henceforth, getting personally involved with him was a trap she'd sidestep at all costs.

* * *

On Wednesday, Mike's sister Sandra stopped by FFU headquarters to pick up some folding chairs and, as an afterthought, invited Sherry out to lunch. When Sherry hesitated, counting up her pennies, she added quickly, "My treat."

Drawn to the slender, dark-haired bride-to-be, and curious to know more about Mike's family in general, Sherry accepted, though it pinched her pride a little to be Sandra's guest. Through no fault of hers, their lunchtime conversation at Selena's in Old Hyde Park, where they split orders of spinach lasagna, salad and garlic toast, centered on Mike. To hear Sandra tell it, though he'd played the field in the past, he'd never been seriously interested in anyone.

"A relationship went bad on him a couple of years ago and, since then, he's kept pretty much to himself," Sandra related. "I might be wrong, but I think he's got a thing for you, Sherry. Sure...I know he's an incorrigible flirt. And that women are crazy about him. Yet I've never heard him talk about anyone the way he talks about you. He's told me more than once how lucky he feels to have landed you for his secretary."

Secretly pleased despite the pledge she'd made to herself not to get tangled up with him, Sherry insisted her luncheon companion was imagining things.

Sandra gave her a Mona Lisa smile. "Maybe so," she agreed. "Only time will tell."

Abruptly changing the subject, she spoke of her wedding, which was coming up in just three days. To Sherry, she didn't seem a bit nervous. "Everyone connected with FFU is coming," Sandra said. "The notice circulated some time ago, so you probably didn't see it. Please consider this your personal invitation. We can expect to see you there, I hope."

Her thoughts once more on money and whether, in good conscience, she could ask her grandmother to baby-sit,

Sherry didn't answer right away. She was slightly startled when Mike's sister reached across the table to squeeze her hand.

"I know what your salary is," Sandra said, "and that you have a baby to support. So please don't even think of bringing a gift. Or hiring someone to watch your baby. Your presence . . . and your little boy's . . . are the only gift I want."

The phone was ringing when Sandra dropped her back at the office. Letting herself in as quickly as she could, Sherry answered breathlessly, "Florida Farmworkers' Union."

"Hi, Sher," Mike's voice said, curling around the stubborn place inside her that missed him like a nice, warm blanket. "How are things going in Tampa, anyway?"

"Umm, pretty well," she managed, not quite trusting the appropriate sounds to come out of her mouth.

To her surprise, after announcing he wouldn't return until Friday evening, Mike seemed somewhat tongue-tied himself. As a result, the silence between them lengthened.

"Actually, I've been thinking about our discussion on the phone last Friday evening, and I don't remember promising not to invite you to a wedding," he said at last. "Sandra's getting married Saturday and, though admittedly it's a little late . . ."

"She invited me this afternoon," Sherry said.

"Well, *good.*" Mike paused, as if considering his next move. "How about going with me?" he suggested. "I need a date. We could classify it as friendship. I promise to behave myself."

Don't do it! You'll only be asking for trouble! her scruples bleated in alarm. You know you want to, the seldom heeded risk-taker in her advised. Whether or not you're willing to admit it, Lisa was a liar. And you're half crazy about him.

The sensible Sherry realized at once that, together with Sandra's, his invitation represented a golden opportunity to size up the rest of Jamie's Ruiz relatives.

"All right," she said, awed by her own casual, almost breezy tone as she decided to accept.

The rest of their conversation revolved around Jamie's reaction to his first day-care experience. As they said goodbye, Sherry was torn between guilt, apprehension and a quivery, elated feeling. Determinedly she focused on practical concerns. I don't have a thing to wear that's even mildly appropriate, she thought as she put down the phone. And no money to buy a new dress.

When Mike arrived to pick them up on Saturday, handsome as sin with a boutonniere adorning his lapel, Sherry was attired in the frock she'd worn beneath her cap and gown at her Leto High School graduation nearly a decade earlier—with a few significant alterations. A semisheer white shadowstripe cotton delicately printed with sprigs of tiny blue flowers, it had originally boasted a demure lace collar and long, full sleeves. Transformed on her grandmother's balky old sewing machine, it had become a glamorous party dress with an off-the-shoulder neckline and tiny puffed sleeves that bared most of her slender arms. In keeping with its mood, she'd tucked a nosegay of bachelor's buttons behind one ear and allowed her usually smooth, chin-length cap of hair to curl romantically about her face.

Catching hold of her hands when she opened the screen door for him, Mike stared down at her without speaking for a moment. How utterly feminine and ladylike she was, without sacrificing an ounce of brains or spirit. He'd never met anyone with such a strong sense of what was morally correct—except perhaps his mother. Yet he didn't doubt for one second that, once reached, her inner woman was both giving and passionate. Though they'd known each other only briefly, he was beginning to have the kind of fantasies about her he'd entertained just once before—with disastrous results.

Of course, Sherry was nothing like the insecure, ultimately unfaithful party girl to whom he'd once contemplated giving his heart, despite a certain superficial resemblance. "You look good enough to eat," he growled, adding with a grin that defused the tension between them, "Don't take that literally. I plan to be a perfect gentleman."

Thanks to Sandra's warmhearted insistence she bring the baby and the fact that Sherry's grandmother was feeling "poorly" that afternoon, they'd be taking Jamie with them. Sherry had decked him out for the occasion in a one-piece sailor suit she'd picked up at a local thrift shop. He looked adorable in it, with his dimpled knees, rosy cheeks and long, dark lashes, as he crawled toward them with the determined force of a miniature locomotive, and attempted to pull himself to a standing position by clutching at Sherry's leg.

With a grin so like his son's that it tore her apart, Mike scooped him up. "How're *you* today, little man?" he said affectionately. "Have you been a good boy for your mommy this week?"

"Jamie's always a good boy, even when he's being Destructo-Baby...aren't you, sweetheart?" Sherry murmured, planting a kiss atop her nephew's dark hair in an effort to conceal her strong upsurge of emotion.

The gesture brought her sufficiently within Mike's orbit that she picked up the scent of his after-shave. God, but he smelled good—all manly moss and spices, which acted as grace notes for his alluring natural scent. Get a grip, she ordered herself. Cozy as it is, letting him escort you to Sandra's wedding, it's strictly playacting with a purpose. Your day of reckoning with Mike Ruiz will arrive sooner than you think.

Holding on to that thought, she snatched up Jamie's diaper bag, urged her sour-faced, disapproving grandmother to get some rest and let Mike lead them out to his freshly waxed convertible. Sandra's wedding would take place in the Ruiz family's parish church and, as they parked near its front steps a short time later, florist's baskets of white gladioli were already in place.

They were an hour and fifteen minutes early. As one of groomsmen, Mike would usher the wedding guests to their seats and generally help out if any minor emergencies occurred.

"Do you want to be seated now?" he asked, resting one hand lightly on Sherry's shoulder. "Or would you rather take Jamie to the parish hall dressing rooms, and have me come for you when the ceremony's about to start? Most of my nieces and nephews will be running around down there, causing untold havoc, while the bride and bridesmaids put on their makeup and assorted relatives carry out their assigned tasks. One more kid isn't going to bother them."

For a bachelor, he certainly had a fair idea of how babies reacted to lengthy confinement, particularly in church. Sherry supposed that was because he'd come from a large family. "The latter, I think," she answered, hoping he wouldn't guess at the little knife-thrusts of pleasure his touch evoked.

Plopped down with her nephew amid the distaff side of his Ruiz relatives, she found herself chattering in a mixture of English and Spanish, accepting effusive compliments on her "precious little boy" and helping baby-sit the other children while their mothers fussed over recalcitrant hairdos and last minute changes of makeup.

Accustomed to a nuclear family that had been decimated by several generations of desertion and premature death, she absorbed the warmth and camaraderie of Mike's female kinsfolk like a sponge. Unlike the women of her family, most of them had living, *present* husbands. Even the ones who didn't seemed less jittery and careworn than Lillian Hayes and what Sherry could remember of her mom. Their common denominator was an air of secure, relaxed contentment.

She was almost sorry her participation in the group had to end when Mike returned to lead her and Jamie to the pew he'd occupy when the service got under way. Something about the stares she got as they took their seats and he gave her hand a little squeeze told her that paying such public attention to a particular woman in front of friends and relatives wasn't usually Mike's style. Ignorant of her plans and whose sister she was, what did he want from her? The question was even more troubling when she inverted it, and applied it to herself.

Chapter Five

Sherry spent most of the wedding service and the Catholic mass that followed it out of doors, chasing butterflies with Jamie in her arms and reading softly to him from his favorite cloth book on the church's front steps. His spontaneous comments, in the form of piercing "Da-da-da's" and noisily executed raspberries, would have made a mishmash of the proceedings if she'd remained in her pew.

Crazy about weddings since she'd been a preschooler playing bride with a dish towel for a veil, she'd have liked to watch Sandra speak her vows. Yet there were aspects of the ceremony she preferred to miss. Thanks to Jamie's need to be entertained, Mike wouldn't be able to reach for her hand during the ceremony. She wouldn't be forced to hold back tears during the sentimental parts for fear of looking foolish. Or struggle with the sweet sensation of his thigh pressing against hers through the fabric of his trouser-leg.

Best of all, she wouldn't be tempted to daydream about a wedding of her own, with Mike as the groom. Sure, there was chemistry between them; she'd be a fool to pretend otherwise. But that would be the extent of it. Looking for permanence with a man who didn't know the meaning of the word had been her sister's cross to bear. She didn't plan to make it hers.

She was simply checking out his family as a logical step in the process of winning justice and recognition for her little nephew. Her scruples appeased by the thought, she willingly took her place beside Mike on the church steps a short time later as the newlyweds and their families greeted well-wishers. Smiling in response to a series of introductions, she didn't dwell on the likelihood that most of the wedding guests who knew him regarded her as Mike's latest conquest. She had her hands full dealing with his proximity and teasing, dark-eyed glances as Jamie attempted to wriggle from her grasp.

Another week and I'll be out of his life, looking for a real job, she promised herself as she hoisted the baby higher and absently kissed his rosy cheek. We won't have to see each other unless Jamie's welfare warrants. It was only when the reception got under way in the parish hall and the musical trio his father had hired for the occasion began to play that Sherry began to guess the true nature of her predicament.

"C'mon... let's dance," Mike proposed in his husky voice.

Before she could protest that she had to watch Jamie, Mike's mother held out her arms for him. "Go ahead, dance with my son," Isabel Ruiz encouraged as, unknowingly, she settled her grandson on her lap. "I adore holding babies... especially one who looks so much like Mike did when he was little. I'll never get enough."

To her relief, Mike didn't seem to take much notice of the remarks. Moving to a lively number with the man who'd abandoned her sister was a revelation that shook Sherry to the core. Though their need to touch was minimal, the fluid sensuality of their parallel steps suggested another kind of partnership, one she'd sworn she wouldn't think about.

She couldn't repudiate the sheer elation she felt. To her amazement, it was as if she and Mike had been born to dance together. With him, maneuvers that, in the arms of other men, had left her feeling unschooled and clumsy, flowed like water, silk unraveling from a bolt.

Danger whispered in her ear as the trio segued into a slower, more provocative number. Though their execution of the proper steps was being carried out in full view of several hundred people, that wasn't how it felt. For Sherry, who admittedly lacked experience in such things, it was as if they were alone on the dance floor, making love fully dressed. She could have sworn she felt Mike's heart thudding through the front of his dinner jacket, a warm flush of desire spreading from his cheek to hers. Certainly her pulse was erratic, thanks to the sudden tumescence he pressed against her lower body, the helpless way he enfolded her.

No, she thought. *No*. I can't let myself feel this way—not with a man who brought my sister so much unhappiness.

Yet suppose past events hadn't unfolded the way Lisa had claimed, and she was free to do as she wished? Jamie was Mike's son; there wasn't much doubt of that. But what if Mike wasn't aware of his existence? You knew Lisa better than most people did, a little voice inside her dared to suggest. And you knew she had a problem with the truth. She was fully capable of failing to tell Mike about the baby if in some twisted way it suited her purposes.

Given Lisa's penniless state during the final year of her life, Sherry couldn't imagine what purposes would have taken precedence over asking for his support. Meanwhile, everything that was headlong and willful in her was drawn to Mike—not just because he cared about the downtrodden and seemed capable of affection for Jamie's sake, but for the man himself, with all his flaws and strengths. I *love* him, she realized, little shudders of recognition skidding down her spine. With the kind of love that could make it to forever. Though I can scarcely believe it, he's the one I've been waiting for.

It was Lisa who'd slept with him, Lisa who'd had his baby. She couldn't pick up her sister's foreshortened life and run with it, as if she were participating in a relay race, anymore than she could settle for the kind of affair that appeared to be his stock-in-trade. Like it or not, she was a forever kind of woman. She needed a man who shared her principles and her outlook.

Somehow, she had to get free—disentangle her common sense from what her hormones were telling her and save herself. "Mike, please..." she protested, slowing her footsteps as she started to pull away from him. "We have to cool it. This is your sister's wedding. Your mom shouldn't have to baby-sit."

Expecting him to let go of her immediately, she was both chagrined and charmed when his hands spanned her waist. "You'll have to give me a minute, *querida,*" he informed her with a self-deprecating grin. "I know I promised to behave. But dancing with you turns me on. I'm temporarily indisposed."

He'd called her darling in Spanish, with an unmistakable tartness in his inflection. Unaccustomed to sexual teasing, or discussing erotic matters so straightforwardly with a member of the opposite sex, Sherry blushed. "I wish you wouldn't... feel that way," she stammered.

"Then you'll have to stop being so pretty and shy and sexy."

Unable to come up with a satisfying retort, she bit her lip.

His head tilted slightly to one side, Mike contemplated her innocence. What a breath of fresh air she was! Smart as a whip, yet completely oblivious to her own allure, she was totally unlike most of the women he'd dated. He wanted to make love to her on the spot. If he so much as kissed her in front of his sister's wedding guests, he believed, he'd spoil his chances.

By now, he had himself under control. They could take a breather from the dance floor. "Look," he said. "Some of Sandy's and Tom's friends are getting ready to decorate their car. What do you say we grab Jamie and join them? He ought to get a kick out of all those crepe paper streamers, tin cans and balloons."

Temporarily let off the hook, yet tied to Mike by her newly discovered feelings, Sherry decided to let go and enjoy the rest of the afternoon. If she was lucky, the "love" she felt might turn out to be infatuation. She could only hope. Whatever the case, she'd deal with the complications later, when they were safe at home again and Jamie had been put to bed.

"Suits me if you don't mind waiting a moment," she answered, managing a smile. "I have a feeling Jamie needs a diaper change."

It was a warm day and, when she emerged from the ladies' room with a refreshed and comfortable baby boy in tow, Mike had removed his jacket. In contrast to his heart-rending grin and the snowy white fabric of his dress shirt, his hair looked darker, his skin even more bronzed than usual. A stab of pleasure told her she was sinking, not swimming, in her struggle not to care for him as he ushered them out the door.

For Sherry, the next few hours passed in a blur of euphoria riddled with underlying misgivings as she and Mike helped decorate the newlyweds' car, ate wedding cake and drank champagne, and took a few more turns around the dance floor. While they were dancing, there wasn't any shortage of laps for Jamie. Not yet at an age when shyness might thwart his gregarious nature, he fussed only a little, spending most of his time laughing and playing peekaboo, jingling people's key chains and, in general, captivating everyone.

To Sherry's surprise, he didn't wilt without his customary nap. She'd just picked him up with the intent of checking his diaper again and giving him some juice from a special training cup when the wedding photographer asked them to pose for him.

"I'm supposed to get family portraits of all the guests, if possible," he explained to Mike with a grin. "It'll only take a second. I must say...your little boy is the spitting image of you, sir."

Struck by the irony of his mistake, though she'd have liked to pretend she was Mike's wife and Jamie's mom, Sherry blushed and worried that her dark-haired boss would recall his mother's comments.

Tossing her a look that plainly said, *Play along...what can it hurt?* Mike helped the man position them for his lens. "Smile, Sher," he whispered, giving her shoulders an encouraging squeeze. "This is for Sandy's family album. We want to look our best."

A bit moodier for the experience, Sherry declined to join in the scramble for Sandra's bouquet of white orchids and stephanotis when it was time for the bride to throw it and change into her going-away outfit. Yes, she was single, she assured the wife of Mike's older brother when the well-meaning forty-year-old tried to include her in the traditional free-for-all. She just didn't happen to be in the market for a husband.

Having wished the newlyweds luck, collected Jamie from his latest admirer and said goodbye to everyone, Sherry and Mike left soon afterward. Susceptible to nodding off in the car whenever he was exhausted, Jamie promptly fell asleep.

Though Mike longed to ask Sherry what she was thinking, he held his tongue. At times this afternoon, I felt us getting close, he thought. But each time, she pulled back. I wonder why she doesn't want to get involved with me. Is there something about me she doesn't like or trust? Or is she still yearning after the man who fathered her little boy?

Everything seemed normal as they pulled into her grandmother's sandspur-choked drive. "Mind if I come in for a minute and use the facilities?" Mike asked.

"Be my guest," Sherry answered, sure it was a ploy to extend the afternoon. "I'm sorry I can't ask you to stay. I have quite a few chores to do...."

Her first clue that something was wrong came as she glanced in the direction of the sunporch on her way to tuck Jamie into his crib. Though the TV was flickering, Lillian Hayes wasn't in her usual chair. Maybe she's gone into the kitchen for a snack, Sherry thought. Or lying down. She wasn't feeling well earlier.

"Gram?" she called, as Mike ducked into the tiny bathroom at the end of the hall. "We're home. Where are you?"

There wasn't any answer.

A frown creasing her forehead as Jamie's head lolled sleepily on her shoulder, she quickly searched the frame cottage's four remaining rooms. And found no one. An uneaten lunch of canned soup and crackers had been abandoned on the kitchen counter. A check of Lillian Hayes's bedroom revealed her purse in its customary place on her dresser. She'd never have left without it, Sherry thought. I hope to God something hasn't happened to her....

"My grandmother's missing," she said in a shaken voice when Mike emerged. "She doesn't have a car and I doubt if she'd go out with anyone, the way she's been feeling. I'm not quite sure... what to do."

Mike was quickly frowning, too. "Don't let's panic," he advised, evaluating the situation. "Maybe she left a note."

Still toting Jamie's sleepy little body, Sherry searched the house again—to no avail. There wasn't any note. "Something's wrong...I know it," she told Mike apprehensively. "If anything has happened to her..."

She broke off in midsentence as a neighbor she recognized approached the house and knocked on the screen door. "Miss Tompkins?" the woman called worriedly, then added when she saw Sherry, "Thank goodness you're back. I had to call the emergency medical service for your grandmother. When I dropped by to drop off some cookies, I found her lying on the floor. She'd passed out. I couldn't revive her. I think she's okay now. One of the paramedics said he thought it was a diabetic coma."

A quick call to the EMS confirmed what the neighbor had told them. Lillian Hayes had been admitted to Tampa General Hospital. "She's conscious and resting at the moment," a nurse on her unit told Sherry when she phoned there next. "We have you down as next of kin. You can visit her for a few minutes if you wish."

Steadying Sherry as she put down the receiver and related the news to him, Mike offered to drive her to the hospital.

"What about Jamie?" she asked with a churning feeling in the pit of her stomach.

Mike gently smoothed the sleeping baby's dark hair, so like his own. "Not to worry," he volunteered. "I'll be happy to watch him for you in the waiting room."

By the time they'd arrived at Tampa General, Sherry's grandmother was feeling a little better. Hooked up to a drip of IV fluids and taking nourishment in the form of an artificially sweetened diabetic pudding, she'd raised the headrest of her hospital bed partway so she could watch one of her favorite television shows.

"Sorry to let you down, Sher," she said in her paper-thin, somewhat raspy voice. "It don't look like I'll be able to watch Jamie for a while...even though, now, it's just evenings and weekends. The doc said they're gonna keep me until my diabetes is regulated."

Feeling absurdly guilty that she'd been at Sandra's wedding, dancing with Mike when her grandmother had needed her, Sherry pleaded with her not to worry. "You just rest and get better," she insisted. "I can handle things."

"Let's hope so, gal." The sudden tartness of her comment belying her weary expression, Lillian Hayes gave Sherry a level look. "If you wanna find a real job, the way you planned to do when you graduated college," she added, "maybe you oughta talk to Jamie's daddy about gettin' some money for him. Every day you wait, things get a little more mixed up. I'd hate to think you was fallin' for him the way Lisa did."

Her grandmother's words all the more painful for their stunning accuracy, Sherry was withdrawn and silent as Mike drove them home. "I'll wait while you put Jamie to bed, okay?" he asked with obvious concern as he switched off the Mustang's engine and saw them to the door.

Choosing the path of least resistance, Sherry nodded in the affirmative. I'd like nothing better than to lean on him . . . feel his strength supporting me, she thought as she put on her nephew's jammies and kissed him good-night. Regrettably it's a luxury I can't afford. Somehow, I have to stay focused.

To her relief, Mike hadn't overheard her grandmother's surname at the hospital and begun asking awkward questions. Yet if she did what the older woman and her own conscience were urging her to do, she realized, he'd be asking them soon enough. It went without saying that he'd be furious when he learned the truth—doubly so because she'd been working for him under false pretenses. The fact that they'd socialized would only exacerbate the situation.

If Lisa had been telling the truth, and he'd dumped her with the full knowledge that she was pregnant, he might also feel trapped by Sherry's demands. As she'd gotten to know him, though, that outcome had seemed less and less plausible. Nobody could fake liking kids as much as he did, whatever his qualifications as husband material. It followed that, if Lisa *hadn't* told him about Jamie and Sherry had perpetuated that omission, he'd have every right to be incensed.

Either way, I lose him, she sighed, running her hands through her hair in frustration. Of course, it wasn't possible to lose what you'd never had in the first place.

Mike was waiting for her in the living room. He got to his feet as she entered, making it clear he didn't expect to hang around. "Look," he said, his hands for once hanging awkwardly at his sides, "if there's anything I can do...

Sherry shook her head. "There really isn't. You've been a big help already...." Pausing, she reconsidered as a thought surfaced. "Actually, you *could* call Jerry Suarez about my car," she suggested.

The grin he gave her hinted he'd deliberately failed to press the issue, no doubt so that he could continue to chauffeur her around. "I'll get on it first thing in the morning," he vowed.

It was time to say good-night. Yet for some reason they continued to stand there in Lillian Hayes' shabby, dimly lit living room, just looking at each other. I want to hold her, Mike admitted. The worst she can do is kick me out for getting fresh. Besides, in his opinion Sherry could *use* a hug. She had so many responsibilities.

He'd keep it brief and nonthreatening. "C'mere," he said, his voice a low growl as he reached for her.

Tears she couldn't quell stung Sherry's eyelids as she allowed herself the respite of his embrace. It was like coming home to a place of safety she hadn't realized existed for her. A moment later, he was gone, after first promising he'd phone her the following afternoon to see how things were going.

Watching from inside the screen door until his taillights had disappeared, she returned to the tiny bedroom she shared with her baby nephew. Sleeping the sleep of innocence, Jamie lay curled on his side with his thumb in his mouth. The long, dark lashes he'd inherited from Mike lightly brushed his cheeks.

"I don't know what we're going to do, pumpkin," Sherry told him with a disconsolate shake of her head as she gently rearranged his bedcovers. "Despite my best efforts not to let it happen, I'm in love with your daddy. And, if I tell him about you, we'll be at each other's throats."

Chapter Six

They hadn't socialized much with Hector at the wedding, though they'd shared a toast with him and his new wife, a recent arrival from Cuba who spoke little English. Several times during the reception, particularly when she and Mike were dancing together, Sherry had caught him watching them. Did we manage to offend him somehow? she wondered when she arrived at the office on Monday and got a distinctly aloof "hello" from him.

Mike wasn't in yet.

"Anything wrong?" she asked, hanging up her jacket in the metal locker that served them as a closet, and placing her purse and sack lunch under her desk.

Hector shrugged. He put down his coffee cup. "Maybe you can tell me," he said.

Did he know something about her relationship to Lisa? Jamie's parentage? "I don't understand," she hedged.

Mike's second in command took his time about answering. "I get the impression you've got too much talent...maybe too much education...to be working this job," he said at last. "I wonder why you're doing it. *Pero,* it's none of my business."

"I'm working this job because I have a baby to support," Sherry snapped.

Turning her back on him, she busied herself typing a report Mike wanted. *If Hector knows something, or even suspects, that means I've got to tell Mike about Jamie sooner than I planned,* she realized.

A few minutes later, Hector left on a fact-finding mission to Immokalee. Shortly thereafter, Sherry's attention was diverted by the arrival of an extremely thin, ragged-appearing black youth. Polite to the point of diffidence, the youth spoke broken English with a heavy French accent.

"This ees place for migrants, *non?*" he asked. "I am migrant. Very hoongry."

It was clear to Sherry that he hadn't eaten for several days. "I have a peanut butter sandwich and an orange, plus a few celery sticks," she offered, handing her lunch bag to him. "If that's not enough, we can get some doughnuts from across the street."

Accepting her offer with painful alacrity, the youth wolfed down Sherry's lunch to the last crumb, polishing off the doughnuts she ran out to buy for him as if he hadn't previously eaten a bite. When his most severe hunger pangs had been assuaged, she was able to get a few facts out of him. His name was Armand Gascoigne and he was thirteen years old. Haitian-born, the son of migrants currently indentured because of an unpaid food and housing bill in one of the most notorious "holdout" camps Mike had described to her, he'd run away after a clash with its sadistic overseer three days earlier.

"I no want to get *mes parents* in trouble wid' heem, so I go," the boy said. "*S'il vous plaît, mad'moiselle,* no send me back 'dere."

Unwilling to promise anything before talking with Mike, Sherry asked if the foreman had injured him. Shyly he showed her several nasty-looking welts and bruises. She was trying to decide whether she ought to take him to a doctor when Mike walked in the door.

At first, Mike didn't pay much attention to the youth who was scrounging doughnut remains from a sack at Sherry's desk. He'd phoned her the day before, as promised, drawing out the conversation until he'd run out of excuses to take up her time. But he hadn't *seen* her. He wanted to rest his eyes on her, to touch her.

"I finally managed to get in touch with Jerry Suarez," he said, standing a little too close to her chair. "Your wheels will be ready this afternoon."

Anxious as she'd been to get her car back, Sherry's tone was serious, impatient. "That's great, Mike. Listen...I think you ought to talk with this young man. He ran away from Brumpton Groves after a fight with the overseer...."

In a heartbeat, Mike was all business. Requesting that Sherry record their conversation, he ushered them into his office and thoroughly questioned the boy. The tale he told was an electrifying one. Unlike most modern groves, which treated their itinerant workers fairly, Brumpton sounded like a hotbed of abuses.

Mike tended to agree with Sherry that Armand needed medical treatment. He considered the fact that the boy was a runaway. His parents would almost certainly be worried about him. Still, he didn't relish the thought of turning him in to the authorities. If he did that, Armand might be returned to the camp, where he'd almost certainly be subjected to reprisals.

Speculating aloud that Armand's parents were probably worried about him, he gauged the boy's reaction.

"No call 'de po'leez," the youngster begged.

Mike shook his head a bit severely. "We have to check the missing person reports."

Brumpton Groves was situated in Morgan County, a central Florida jurisdiction. While Sherry phoned one of

Mike's contacts in its sheriff's department, Mike ran the boy over to a nearby clinic and had his wounds dressed. No one had filed a report related to his disappearance, it seemed. Weighing the pros and cons, Mike came to a tentative decision. He'd ask his brother Joe and sister-in-law Kathy, who had four children of their own, to keep Armand for a few days.

"Kathy's coming by to pick him up," he told Sherry a few minutes later. "Meanwhile, something's got to be done about that place. I'm calling an emergency board meeting...."

That evening, Marta Ramirez arranged to keep Jamie a few hours later than usual so Sherry could take notes at the hastily called session. The discussion proved hot and heavy. Though she didn't let on, she was greatly distressed by what Mike had in mind. To her horror, he wanted to go under-cover—pretend to be a migrant worker and document firsthand the conditions Armand had described. It was the kind of exploit that would get the camp noticed, maybe even elicit some corrective action on the part of the local political establishment.

She didn't need the board members' warnings to tell her such a stunt would be dangerous. Mike could get beaten up. Or worse. The move might prompt a tangle of lawsuits.

"I'm willing to take my chances if we can clean up that place," Mike averred.

In the end, no final decision was reached. Mike had the board members' tentative approval, provided he did some checking first, and got back to them with the information. Before heading out to Morgan County, though, he needed their final okay. In any event, since he'd committed to a three-day stay in Tallahassee, beginning around noon the following day, and the church picnic to benefit FFU was coming up that weekend, it looked as if several weeks might elapse before any action could be undertaken.

In the interim, Mike would get one of his friends in Morgan County to search quietly for Armand's parents. It was possible they hadn't remained at Brumpton. If not, maybe they could be located, and the family reunited.

To Sherry, the necessary delay in carrying out Mike's undercover operation was cold comfort. Eventually he'd get his way, as he usually did. And something bad would happen to him. She worked up the courage to tell him what she thought as he drove her over to Jerry Suarez's place to pick up her little compact. "I wish you'd reconsider about going undercover," she told him.

He shot her a speculative look. "Why do you say that?"

"Because it's dangerous. You could get hurt."

Was it possible she cared for him? Or would she have felt the same concern for anyone who came within her orbit? "It's sweet of you to worry," he answered, hoping it was the former. "But I'm a big boy. I can handle it."

Tempted to argue, Sherry dropped the subject as they reached Jerry Suarez's modest concrete block house and the detached triple-bay garage where he repaired automobiles. She couldn't linger, as she still had to pick up Jamie.

"Thanks for the ride . . . and your help in getting my car fixed," she said, reaching for the door handle. "I really appreciate it. Have a safe trip to Tallahassee. I'll see you on Friday, I suppose."

Saturday too, if he got his wish. But he wouldn't ask her yet. "*De nada*. Don't work too hard," he answered with a grin as he shifted the Mustang into gear and headed home to pack his clothes.

During the next few days, the worry Hector had prompted with his questions returned to haunt Sherry again and again. She'd have to tell Mike about Jamie, and soon, before he found out from some other source.

Try as she would, she couldn't predict his reaction. Stupefaction followed by anger, she guessed. For starters, the knowledge would probably nip their blossoming friend-ship in the bud. While that couldn't be allowed to matter in the larger scheme of things, she realized it might also mean a suit for Jamie's full-time custody.

Though she'd loved her nephew from the moment of his birth, she hadn't been as close to him initially, given the necessity of completing her course work in Gainesville. Following her graduation, though, and the steady decline of her grandmother's health, she'd become progressively more involved in his care, until now it almost seemed that they were joined at the hip. She didn't think she could bear to be parted from him, no matter how much he compli-cated the life she'd planned for herself.

The truth was, since returning from school and spend-ing more time with him, she'd begun to love him less like an aunt and more like a mother. *It's as if he grew in my womb instead of Lisa's,* she realized. *I love him that much.*

Similar thoughts were cascading through her head when Mike phoned the office on Thursday.

"Hi, how's tricks?" he asked without preamble, sound-ing as if he was in something of a rush.

Sherry's heart turned over at the husky resonance of his voice. Unluckily for her, Mike was someone *else* she was beginning to care about too much. "Good," she an-swered, cautiously maintaining her composure. "What's up?"

"I was wondering if we could see each other this week-end." He paused. "I know I promised we'd stick to being friends. It can still be that way if you want. It's just that I can't stop thinking about you."

Caught off guard by his directness, she faltered. "You mean . . . date?"

"Is that such a radical notion?"

In point of fact, it wasn't. She'd been moving toward it herself for several weeks. *The further I let things slide in this direction, the bigger the debt I'll have to pay the piper,* she warned herself. Of course, I could use the occasion as a chance to tell him about Jamie, and get it over with. Meanwhile, the flesh was weak. She'd have to make sure the Sherry who wanted Mike on any terms didn't lure them into any compromising situations.

"I suppose it'd be okay," she answered slowly, "provided we didn't go somewhere we couldn't take a baby."

Mike was one step ahead of her. "What I had in mind was the church picnic," he said innocently. "They're busing everyone over to the beach at Howard Park. Of course, we can drive ourselves and leave whenever we want, once I've given my speech and done the requisite mingling. Jamie ought to love it. All you need to do is bring yourself, some silverware and a blanket or tablecloth . . .and bask in the success of your efforts."

A helpless feeling washing over, Sherry resigned herself to her fate. She'd attend the picnic with Mike, allow herself a few fantasies about making a life with him and 'fess up about Jamie's parentage before saying goodnight. Insofar as her personal interests were concerned, the chips could fall where they might. It was *Jamie's* interests that mattered. By now, there wasn't much doubt in her mind that Mike would be a good father to him. The only question left to resolve was whether he'd agree to share custody. Unselfishly speaking, she ought to be glad that, after spending nearly a year in the world without either of his parents being involved in his upbringing, her little nephew would finally get the recognition and financial support he deserved.

At the church picnic organized to benefit the Florida Farmworkers' Union, Mike unconsciously shoved the knife of Sherry's ambivalence in a little deeper by toting Jamie around like a dad showing off his prize kid. Over and over, as he made the rounds expressing his gratitude, talking up FFU's activities and relating the need for better migrant services, people mistook them for a family. With his big, brown eyes and dark hair, Jamie was referred to repeatedly as his spitting image. "A chip off the old block," one man called him, offering the baby a balloon on a string to grasp.

The slanting, amused looks Mike gave her each time it happened only deepened her embarrassment. Yet, at the same time, they aroused a kind of fabricated hope. What if he asked me to marry him? she fantasized. And agreed to adopt Jamie? All my objectives would be fulfilled. He'd never need to know the truth.

Ethical questions aside, her perception of reality was severely at odds with such a scenario. For one thing, Mike wasn't the marrying kind. Her sister's experience with him had proven that. He might desire her the way he'd desired Lisa and God knew how many other women who'd figured in his past. But he wouldn't want to curtail his freedom for her sake.

He'd have to know for other reasons, too. If by some unforeseen caprice of chance, they *did* get together, she couldn't very well keep her relationship with Lisa secret. Someone who had known both her and her sister was bound to happen along. Plus her legal claim to Jamie as his aunt and not his mother wasn't the best. It'd be bound to come up if Mike wanted to adopt him. She'd be just as caught in her own web.

There was also the matter of her virginity vis-à-vis Mike's belief that she'd conceived and given birth. Imagine his surprise, she thought, taunting herself with the irony of it, if we got around to a wedding night and he found I was still untouched.

She'd have to tell him whose son Jamie really was. I'll do it tonight, she decided, biting the bullet. On the porch swing at Gram's after Jamie's been put to bed. And try to ride out the storm that's sure to follow in the hope he'll see reason. Surely when he cools down, he'll realize my intentions were the best. How could I have known he'd turn out to be the kind of person he is if I hadn't checked him out?

She got some respite from her thoughts during a series of picnic-oriented games that included several sack races, a rousing volleyball contest and a relay race. Once again, there was no shortage of grandmotherly laps for Jamie to occupy, so she had a chance to participate.

The relay race, which required competing lines of picnic-goers to pass a half dozen fresh oranges from one person to another without the use of their hands turned out to be particularly erotic in their case. Wriggling against Mike as she tried to transfer one of the oranges from beneath her chin to his, she could feel her nipples tighten. The sensation put all sorts of ideas into her head.

The sun was slanting through the trees, throwing a lengthening pattern of shadows against the grass, by the time everyone had spread blankets on the ground or arranged their cloths and silverware atop picnic tables. As a means of raising money for FFU, the food and soft drinks for the picnic had been catered by the church's social-action committee. For some time, Sherry had been smelling the tantalizing aroma of baked beans and her favorite barbecued chicken. She, Mike and Jamie were part of the line that quickly formed when the event chairman rang her dinner bell and called on everyone to fill their plates.

With Jamie's comfort in mind, Sherry had decided they'd eat on a blanket. More interested in a toddler on the next blanket than he was in eating, he kept trying to escape and go exploring on his hands and knees. Inevitably, his rompers were smudged with grass stains.

"All boy, aren't you, and anxious to be about your business in the world?" Mike teased with a grin, hauling him back yet another time and then holding him comfortably by the hands so he could stand upright. Crowing with delight, Jamie took several assisted steps.

Before Sherry's very eyes, her sister's baby was growing up. What if Mike took him away, and she couldn't be on hand to celebrate the little triumphs of his babyhood, or comfort his infant tears? She'd be losing something infinitely precious.

"He loves that game," she remarked wistfully, watching father and son together. "At home, he pulls himself up and hangs on to the furniture as leverage to get wherever he wants to go. He'll be walking on his own any day now. Only last week, I bought him his first pair of hard-soled shoes..."

"Let's see if he wants to walk now," Mike suggested. "Scooch over on the blanket a little, Sher, and hold out your hands to him."

More sentimental about what was happening than she cared to admit, Sherry did as he asked. In response, Mike lightly spanned the baby's midsection, leaving Jamie's chubby little hands free to reach for hers.

"Okay, kiddo," he prodded. "Go for it."

"C'mon, sweetheart," she chimed in. "Come to Sherry."

His hands still framing the baby's middle, Mike shot her a surprised and puzzled look. "You're not teaching him to call you 'mommy'?" he asked.

She didn't hear the question. By pure happenstance, Jamie had chosen that moment for his first stroll. Taking one and then two more tottering, unaided steps, he clutched at Sherry's outstretched hands and collapsed, giggling, into her lap. "Good boy!" she exclaimed, scooping him up and covering him with kisses. "What a little athlete you are! I'm so proud of you!"

"Excuse me, Mr. Ruiz..."

The blond, forty-something speaker was the church's social-action chairman, who had masterminded the picnic. Apologizing for cutting short their play session with Sherry's baby, she wanted to remind Mike it was almost

time for his speech. The request drove Sherry's odd remark from his head.

"Of course," he said, flashing her his celebrated smile as
he got to his feet. "It's my pleasure to talk before such a
caring, concerned group."

As Sherry watched from her blanket with a somewhat
more subdued baby boy in her lap, playing with his plastic
"ring of keys," Mike's speech about the needs of migrant
workers received rapt attention. Twice his remarks earned
bursts of sustained applause. She couldn't keep feelings of
melancholy at bay as she listened. What a change there's
been in my attitude toward Mike, she thought, biting her
lip. When I first set eyes on him at the university, I had a
terrible opinion of him. Now it would break my heart to
arouse his anger. Or suffer his indifference.

Yet in a way she couldn't fully explain, she was happy at
that moment. Proud of his ability to sway his listeners, she
wouldn't have missed the picnic for the world. When he
finished and offered to take questions, she wanted to ap-
plaud longer and more loudly than anyone.

Following the question-and-answer session that wrapped
up his presentation, Mike circulated a little more, winning
numerous promises of future involvement in his cause. By
the time he returned to the blanket he'd shared with Sherry
and Jamie, it was after 6:00 p.m. Beginning to glow pink
and magenta with the approaching sunset, a magnificent
display of clouds was reflected in the calm waters of the
Gulf of Mexico and the small lagoon that bordered their
picnic area. Still clutching his plastic baby keys, a very tired
little boy had curled up in Sherry's lap. He was fast asleep.

"Let's not disturb him for a few minutes," Mike said,
sinking down beside her. "I'd like to unwind a bit...sit here
with my arm around you before we have to go."

Afraid it would be her last chance to savor that kind of
intimacy with him, Sherry let him draw her close. She
didn't object when his mouth teased hers in a light kiss.

Because of their surroundings, the kiss didn't turn passionate. On the next blanket, the older siblings of the toddler Jamie had noticed earlier were giggling. Though she didn't turn her head and look, she was willing to bet their parents—along with most of the other church members who'd given Mike such an enthusiastic hearing—were gazing indulgently in their direction.

The park closed at dusk, and soon it was time for them to go. As they started back to Tampa beneath a sky still streaked with light, their newfound harmony seemed all the sweeter because it was suffused with regret.

I don't want to tell him whose son my little boy is, and admit I've been investigating him from the start, she thought, giving her head a little shake. I'd rather go on pretending I'm Jamie's birth mom—that I never had a sister named Lisa. But loyalty to her nephew and his dead mother wouldn't let her. She'd have to level with Mike, even if that meant emotional disaster for herself.

Perhaps because of her strong reluctance to see it end, their trip across the bay seemed the shortest in memory. She barely had time to firm her resolve before Mike was parking outside her grandmother's house.

"I'll hold Jamie while you unlock the door," he offered.

The house was shadowy and quiet without the yellow glow of her grandmother's reading lamp, the background noise that usually flowed from the older woman's television set. Before departing for Howard Park, Sherry had left several windows open to catch the breeze. As a result, the threadbare, painfully neat rooms smelled of fresh-cut grass from the yard next door.

How wonderful it would be to put Jamie down for the night secure in the knowledge I'd nestle with Mike between freshly laundered sheets, she thought. Make love to him the way I've read about it in books. And fall asleep in his arms. Sadly, though he, too, was probably thinking about bed, he wasn't the sort of man to offer her a commitment. She'd consider herself lucky if he was still speaking to her by the end of the evening.

Transfixed by her thoughts, Sherry had hesitated in the living room, as if she wasn't sure of her next step. Still holding Jamie, Mike had paused too. "Where do you want him?" he asked, his strong, beautifully shaped hands expertly cuddling the baby against his shoulder.

"On my bed, for starters." Speaking in a whisper, she led the way into her Spartan sleeping quarters and switched on a night-light. "I'll have to change him again before I tuck him in," she explained. "If we're extra quiet, maybe he won't wake up completely and start to fuss...."

Mike shrugged, clearly undaunted by the prospect. "We can always rock him back to sleep on the porch swing if he does," he suggested.

He was so easygoing, so tolerant of an infant. He seemed so comfortable handling one. No doubt the ease carried over from time spent with his nieces and nephews. Yet as she exchanged a clean diaper for Jamie's soiled one and substituted terry cloth jammies for his grass-stained rompers, Sherry knew his interaction with them couldn't totally account for it.

His inability to remain faithful to a single woman notwithstanding, the man was daddy material. He exuded the necessary warmth, made all the right moves. She'd seen Jamie respond to him. Though she still had a host of questions about what had transpired between him and Lisa, she no longer doubted her nephew would benefit from knowing him as a parent.

Perhaps because she'd missed the guidance of both parents during her growing-up years, she didn't like to think of Mike raising him alone—even from an unselfish standpoint. Babies needed mommies *and* daddies. She was the closest thing Jamie had to the former. As he grew and changed and gradually ventured forth in the world, he'd need her to kiss away the ~~hurts~~ as much as he needed Mike to roughhouse with him.

The simple fact was, he needed them both. Maybe, just maybe, she could make Mike see that, despite the hurt and anger he was sure to feel over her mistrust of him. If so, he might not sue for exclusive custody. She could only hope.

Tucking her nephew into his crib beneath a light blanket and kissing his rosy cheek, she straightened and switched off the lamp. "Let's go sit on the porch," she said, turning to the dark-haired man who waited just inches from where she stood. "We need to talk."

What did she have in mind? Mike wondered as their gazes caught and held. Would she air a multitude of second thoughts about dating him because he was her boss? Give a tight little speech about how nice he was and announce in the next breath that she was still hung up on the guy who'd gotten her pregnant?

Whatever the case, he didn't want to *talk* to her. He wanted to kiss her until they were both reeling with it, and she didn't give a damn for the phony barriers that separated them.

They were a breath apart in the darkened bedroom she shared with her son. Bridging the gap with a sigh that spoke of his growing inability to keep his hands to himself where she was concerned, Mike reached for her. His mouth descended on hers like an avalanche.

The explosive fervor of his kiss nearly blew Sherry away. It was as if, symbolically, a match had been struck, the carbon-and-sulphur tip representing her pent-up longing hissing into a bright, unquenchable flame. From the depths of her womanhood, she longed to mate with him—fuse herself inextricably with the person he was. Igniting like the fuse to a cache of dynamite, the same wanton craving spread from the exploratory fingertips he'd inserted beneath her blouse to the depths where she needed him most.

She'd never lain with a man. Never felt one seeking in that most private of places. Yet how could she deny him entry? He was her mate, her counterpart, the longed-for *other* she was destined to know as intimately as herself.

He was also Mike Ruiz, the Cuban-American lawyer who'd impregnated her sister, a man she'd initially despised and still considered an emotional risk. Though her antipathy had metamorphosed into affection, she owed him the truth about Jamie, not the betrayal of her most cherished principles.

"Mike...we can't do this," she protested, struggling to free herself from his embrace.

He refused to cooperate in her deliverance. "What's wrong, Sher?" he demanded, the rough-hewn quality of his voice tugging at her already troubled emotions. Shakily she stood her ground. "I'm not going to sleep with you."

By now, he was holding her tightly, yet Sherry knew a word could free her. "Why not, if it would please us both?" he asked.

A flood tide of warmth lit Sherry's cheeks. Had she been that obvious? "I don't want to get involved," she whispered.

Confused and subliminally aware he didn't have all the puzzle pieces, Mike fought for clarity. "Why not?" he persisted. "Are you still in love with the man who fathered your baby? Or just afraid you'll get pregnant again, out of wedlock?"

Cut to the quick by his frank statement of what he saw as the problem, Sherry bristled. "You don't know my life story!"

"So, tell it to me."

"Maybe I will...someday."

"You ought to know I'd protect you, Sher. That I'd never put you in the position he did."

The irony of his statement was all but unbearable, given the outcome of Lisa's affair with him. Sustaining it like a blow to the softest part of her stomach, she didn't answer.

"I swear to God," he added, "the way you act whenever I try to touch you...if I didn't know better, I'd think you were a virgin. Yet you're the mother of an eleven-month-old baby."

In her agitated state, it seemed to Sherry that he was mocking everything she held dear. Pride rose up and choked her. "No, I'm not," she contradicted him.

Mike stared. "What are you talking about?"

She hadn't wanted to tell him that way, spilling her guts in the heat of an argument. Yet perhaps she didn't have to divulge everything. "You may as well know the truth," she revealed, each word a death knell to their relationship as she'd known it. "While I consider myself Jamie's mother, I didn't give birth to him."

Chapter Seven

Mike felt as if he'd stumbled into the plot of a science fiction movie. Sherry was speaking English—one of two languages he'd learned as a small child. Yet nothing she'd said had made any sense to him. "Maybe we'd *better* go out on the porch and talk," he said.

Leaving Jamie to sleep the sleep of innocence in his crib, Sherry led the way to her grandmother's sagging wooden swing. The chains that suspended it from the porch ceiling creaked in protest at the weight of their bodies, but she didn't notice. At the moment, all her attention was focused on the man she could feel herself losing, and the troubled frown that drew his brows together.

He was the first to speak. "I don't mean to pry. But the fact is, I'm curious," he said, slipping into sarcasm in his bewilderment. "Did you adopt Jamie? Or steal him from a baby carriage while his real mother's back was turned?"

Already hurting over the probable outcome of their talk, Sherry felt his opprobrium like a lash. "He's my sister's child," she answered as calmly as she could. "She died of an unsuspected aneurysm when he was two months old. My grandmother took up the slack until I could finish my last year of college and return to Tampa to care for him.''

The confession that she was a college graduate barely registered. Mike was too busy feeling like a complete idiot. Instead of giving birth to an illegitimate child—no crime, certainly—Sherry had taken responsibility for her sister's baby. Though the commitment was a major one, tying her down when she might have chosen a more carefree lifestyle as a pretty, independent woman, it was plain she didn't view him as a burden. Her strong maternal love for him shone in her every word and gesture. Meanwhile, defused though it was of its emotional content for him, the issue of Jamie's father and the support he owed the boy still needed to be raised, in his opinion.

Firmly separate on her side of the swing, Sherry stared off into the trees. Was she fighting back tears? If so, he had himself to blame. He'd been unnecessarily rough on her.

''Sher...forgive me for spouting off to you the way I did,'' he apologized after a moment. ''You did nothing to deserve that kind of treatment. All I can say is that I admire what you're doing. If possible, I'd like to help. You don't seem to be getting much assistance from Jamie's father. With my credentials as lawyer, I could rattle his cage for you...sue him for punitive damages in addition to back support if he doesn't cooperate. I wouldn't charge you a penny for my services.''

Sherry's urge to weep intensified. God, but things had gotten complicated. By her clumsy amateur investigation of him, she'd brought Mike to the point of offering to sue himself. She doubted if he'd thank her for it when he learned the tangled truth.

''You'd better hear the rest of the story before advising me,'' she whispered.

There was something hidden, something that would shock about what she'd tell him. With the unerring instinct that had served him brilliantly during his days as a trial lawyer and continued to ease his way as an activist, Mike sensed it involved him.

But that was crazy. How could it?

"Okay," he responded, deliberately softening the edge he could feel creeping into his tone. "I'm listening."

From the depths of her soul, Sherry longed for the moment to pass. *I could lie,* she thought. *Tell him Lisa didn't know the father's name, or pretend she refused to tell me.*

The sister she'd been and the mother she'd become for Jamie's sake wouldn't let her evade the truth. Pulling at a loose thread that would unravel quickly to the center of her tale, she turned in the velvety darkness that surrounded them to look at him.

"As you already know," she said, "my last name's Tompkins. My parents died in a seven-car pileup on the expressway when I was three years old. But my mom was never married to the man who fathered my older half sister. As a result, Lisa inherited Mom's maiden name, which was the same as Gram's..."

"Lisa?" Mike echoed. Uneasy furrows rumpling his forehead, it occurred to him that he and Sherry's grandmother hadn't been properly introduced.

Her heart sinking at the possibility Lisa might have been right about him, Sherry nodded. At least she'd know. "Her name was Lisa Hayes," she said, watching his beautiful eyes widen. "I take it you remember her."

Would Mike ever forget? Slender and effervescent, with a wide, infectious smile and curly, bleached-blond hair, Lisa Hayes had knocked his socks off. She'd made him laugh, called forth the same protective quality Sherry evoked in him. Briefly, he'd contemplated giving up his bachelorhood for her.

That is, he had until...

"You're Lisa's *sister?*" he asked incredulously, leaning forward to study her face. "You don't look a bit like her...except maybe around the jawline. And the eyebrows."

At least he wasn't denying the possibility such a connection could exist. "I favor my father, if family photographs are any indication," she said, waiting for the truth to hit. A moment later, it did. He and Lisa Hayes had carried on a torrid, two-month affair before he'd quit her cold. Anything was possible, though they'd used birth control. They could have made a child together.

Hesitating, he called up his mental image of Jamie. "You actually think Jamie's my son?" he asked.

Don't you want him to be? Sherry retorted silently. I'd give anything if he were mine instead. To do him justice, the idea was new to him yet.

"What do *you* think?" she said. "He has your eyes. Your hair. The same impudent grin. Don't take my word for it. Take Lisa's. She told me she was carrying your child during the final months of her pregnancy. She said..."

Having ultimately come to know Lisa Hayes far better than he'd have liked, Mike doubted the narrative she'd laid on Sherry had been complimentary. Or, for that matter, truthful. Meanwhile, he was reeling at the idea that he had a son. If her precious little boy was really his...

"Maybe you'd better tell me everything," he said.

It was too late, now, to take any other tack. "She said you didn't want to be bothered with a baby," Sherry disclosed. "That you dumped her the moment you learned she was pregnant."

Tough guy that he was, Mike winced. "Well, she was right about who did the dumping, at least," he growled. "If what you're saying is true, how come she didn't ask me for child support?"

As she'd put forward her sister's claim, Sherry's sense of outrage had reasserted itself. Mike's blunt acknowledgement that he'd been the one to call things off, together with his none-too-subtle implication that Lisa had been a liar, only added fuel to the fire. She didn't stop to consider the fact that he hadn't corroborated Lisa's assertions.

"Why do you *suppose?*" she snapped. "Can you really blame her for refusing to beg someone who rejected her for help? Of course, in my opinion, it wouldn't have been begging. She'd simply have been demanding what was hers... and Jamie's... by right."

His expression grim, Mike thought about the last time he'd seen Lisa Hayes. The mental picture his recollection drew wasn't a pretty one. Jamie, on the other hand, was a different story. In the short time since he'd met Sherry, Mike had become thoroughly enamored of the active, dark-haired child he'd believed to be her son. Playing with Jamie and watching Sherry interact with him had made him think how nice it would be to have a family—father a child of his own.

Now she was telling him the boy was his. Though part of him recoiled at the idea of being connected, through an infant's inextricably linked genes, with a woman he preferred to forget, in his heart of hearts, he wanted to celebrate. He had a little boy! His rational self realized the likely date of Jamie's conception supported Sherry's contention. If he and Lisa had conceived a child during their two-month affair, he or she would be about Jamie's age. I don't understand how it could have happened, he thought. We used birth control. Of course, it isn't foolproof....

If Jamie was his son, then he had a right to him. By not telling him about the boy's existence, Lisa, Sherry and her grandmother had done him a great disservice.

"Why didn't you approach me with this information earlier?" he asked. His tone added, "There'd better be a damn good explanation."

Wide-eyed, Sherry stuttered in her surprise. "But...but... you told Lisa you didn't want him! How was I supposed to know..."

Like a plague of locusts primed to devour everything in sight, Mike's anger was settling in, overwhelming the confused joy he felt. "I didn't say anything of the sort," he shot back. "How could I have, when she didn't tell me she was pregnant? During our affair, brief as it was, your sister lived at my West Shore apartment. I kicked her out when I came home early from an out-of-town meeting one night and found her with another guy in my bed."

Sherry's face flamed as if *she* had committed the offense in question. "I don't believe you," she answered, ignoring a gut-level reaction that, in her half sister's repertoire, such behavior had probably been typical.

"Believe what you like."

The swing pitched wildly as Mike got to his feet with the express purpose of putting some distance between him and Sherry so he could think. Steadying it with an abrupt gesture that threatened to put a crick in her neck, he paused to consider yet another unanswered question.

"Given your relationship to Lisa and your probable opinion of me, I'd be interested in knowing your purpose for coming to work for me," he challenged. "Ditto your acceptance of my personal invitations."

By now, Sherry was on her feet as well. Ironically, her plan had succeeded. She'd gotten close—investigated him without arousing his suspicions and learned enough to set her mind at rest. She felt certain he'd make Jamie a good father—all the more so if he'd been speaking the truth when he'd insisted Lisa had never told him they were going to be parents.

So why did she feel so heartsick?

That's easy, she thought, answering her own question. I love him. And we're history. Whatever chance I had with him has gone up in smoke.

"Because of what Lisa told me, I felt I had to check you out," she said. "I couldn't think of a better, more cost-efficient way to do it than to get a job with your organization. As for the personal invitations..."

He waited.

"They started out to be the same thing. But..."

Mike had heard enough. "I need a secretary," he said. "And I feel you have some obligation to me. Until we sort things out, I'll expect you to fulfill your commitment."

A moment later, he was gone. As she watched the Mustang's taillights recede in the distance, Sherry was left with nothing but questions. Would he sue for custody? Or blow off his responsibility? Demand tests?

Despite the strong resemblance between himself and Jamie, he could hardly be blamed for wanting proof if Lisa had been sleeping around on him. It remained to be seen whether he'd share access to Jamie, or fight any attempt on the part of Lisa's family to share in his upbringing. If I know Mike, he'll demand full parental rights, she thought as the taillights vanished and she went into the house with an aching heart.

The little boy who'd become hers by virtue of attrition and her loving care for him was asleep on his stomach, his diaper-padded bottom humping the air. Unique and precious, he'd leave a gaping hole in her life if his father took him away from her—just as losing Mike himself would. I shouldn't have told him, she thought, wiping away a tear before it could fall on the baby's cheek. If I hadn't, maybe I could have kept them both.

Several hours later, as Sherry paced the floor of her grandmother's living room, unable to sleep, Mike showed up in a West Tampa tavern popular with the Hispanic community. He was quaffing beer and throwing darts at a corkboard target with vicious accuracy when Hector walked in.

"I saw your car outside. Have a fight with your girlfriend?" his second in command asked with a turned-down lip.

Mike's expression was thunderous. "None of your business," he retorted.

"It's bad, huh? *Recuerdas,* I told you..."

Stunned and tentatively overjoyed that he might be Jamie's father, yet skeptical the boy was really his, Mike was furious at being the target of Sherry's investigation. He'd fallen hard for her. And she'd led him on with an ulterior motive. Still, invited to bash her verbally, he considered himself too raw and confused to exercise good judgement.

"Stuff it, *amigo,*" he replied in a tone that, while faintly conciliatory in opposition to his words, didn't offer Hector any encouragement. "Whatever problems I've got with Sherry Tompkins," he added, "can be solved without your help."

Sunday dragged with the excruciating slowness of wind and rain wearing away a rock. On Monday morning, after dropping Jamie off in day care, Sherry was the first to arrive at FFU headquarters. Though she expected to be fired the moment Mike walked in, despite what he'd said, she made a show of hanging up her suit jacket and brewing coffee before sitting down at her desk. She'd start on the statistical report Mike had handed her to type on his return late Friday. Maybe she could finish it before she received her walking papers.

Hector arrived a few minutes later. From the way he stared at her, she could tell he knew something. Whatever it was, he didn't share it. Mumbling a barely audible "hello," he got busy on the phone. Their backs to each other, they turned toward the door in unison when Mike walked in.

Sherry could see at once that the man she loved still had an enormous chip on his shoulder. His beautiful eyes meeting hers in a searing, accusatory look, he quickly turned away and busied himself doctoring a mug of coffee with too much cream and sugar. Can me if you must, she pleaded silently with his back. But don't embarrass me in front of your friend. Have the courtesy to do it in private.

It was as if he'd heard. "Hector," he said, taking a sip of the saccharine, steaming brew and clearing his throat, "I need to talk to Sherry. Go get yourself a doughnut or something."

His friend's *mestizo* features took on an obdurate look. "I've got calls to make," Hector said. "Your office isn't private enough?"

"Favor que me hace."

Hector glanced in her direction. "Okay. I can make them from the gas station."

A moment later, Sherry and Mike had the place to themselves. Stifling the urge to weep, she faced him without flinching. "If you're going to fire me, get it over with so I can start looking for another job," she said.

Compulsively Mike searched her face for any resemblance to Lisa. He didn't find much. "I'm not going to fire you," he answered. "At least not yet."

She allowed her hands to unclench a little. "What, then?"

"I've, uh, thought long and hard about the matter we discussed on Saturday," he said, refusing to share with her his confused but unfeigned hope that Jamie might really be his son. "I can see just one way out of the impasse in which we find ourselves ... genetic testing. Yes, I know ... you accepted your sister's word that Jamie is my son. You probably still do. *I* don't, without proof, for what I consider to be a very good reason. Since I'll likely be asked to support him until he's eighteen, I feel I'm within my rights requesting it."

As he spoke, he held the warmth that customarily radiated from him like a force field sternly in check. From what Sherry could tell, he seemed to regard fending off the financial challenge Jamie represented as his only objective. How can he be so money-grubbing, so mercenary, she asked herself. Doesn't he realize Jamie's one of the greatest treasures that'll ever come into his keeping? His claim to immortality is wrapped up in those bright baby thoughts, big, brown eyes and chubby fingers.

"I agree...genetic testing's a good idea," she said at last. "Regrettably, I can't afford to pay for it. *Or* to sue you if you don't agree voluntarily to support Jamie. His claim, if he has any, will have to rest on your generosity."

Mike regarded her with narrowed eyes. Was she being facetious? Or merely honest with him? If it was the latter, the discovery that she'd planned to request, not demand, his help would allow him to trust her a little more. Though he longed to believe in the marvel that Jamie might be his, he continued to mistrust it, lest it prove to be a hoax—Lisa's final slap at him.

"I happen to have a friend on the medical staff at Tampa General who's also a genetics professor at USF," he said. "I can almost guarantee he'll do the necessary tissue typing at cost. If it's okay with you, I'll call him right away... set up an appointment."

For Sherry, the waiting would be infinite. Already certain what the tests would prove, she was desperate to know just one thing—whether Mike would try to take the baby away from her.

To her surprise, when she visited her grandmother at the hospital that evening, after arranging with Marta Ramirez to keep Jamie an extra hour, the older woman took the latest developments philosophically. She didn't seem the least bit fearful that they'd lose Jamie over the long run.

"You know and I know Lisa was tellin' the truth when she said Mike Ruiz was her baby's daddy," Lillian Hayes advised from the bedside easy chair where she was sitting to watch a supermarket game show. "So that ain't an issue. From what you say, Jamie'll be all right with him...even if he gets custody and cuts us out of the picture. Pretty soon, the novelty'll wear off. He'll be wantin' to go out on dates with his women friends and need a baby-sitter. Mark my words... he'll be *glad* of an auntie and great-gram to leave his baby with.''

Persuaded though she was that life without Jamie would be like a desert for her, Sherry grimaced inwardly at the thought of caring for him so that Mike could romance other women.

''We'll see,'' she answered, keeping her emotions to herself.

As she left the hospital a short time later to pick up the baby, she let herself cry a few self-indulgent tears and then packed them in. Jamie's my son, too, in the ways that count most, she comforted herself. The question is, can I make Mike see it? To be perfectly honest, perhaps she couldn't. Thoroughly depressed, she was convinced her dream of creating a family unit with Mike and Jamie had slipped beyond her grasp.

Mike arranged for his and Jamie's contributions to the genetic-testing process to be made Wednesday afternoon at the clinic associated with USF's medical school. With the help of a lab technician, he and the baby would provide infinitely tiny tissue samples. The procedure was virtually painless.

Unknown to Sherry, he booked his and Jamie's appointments just twenty minutes apart. They'd barely spoken at the office since their Monday morning conversation and, with tension so thick between them, she'd assumed he'd do otherwise. She almost jumped when he exited one of the examining rooms as she waited to go in with the baby.

Though he paused, his greeting was brief. ''Thanks for coming,'' he said, his eyes flickering from her face to Jamie's and back again. ''Do you plan to return to the office this afternoon?''

Had he changed his mind about firing her? Bracing herself for a jolt, she answered in the affirmative.

Delivered just seconds before he strode out of the clinic, his response was all business. "Good," he said gruffly. "I've got some letters to write. I'm going to need your help."

Two weeks to the day later, the test to determine Jamie's parentage came back positive. The boy was Mike's son, as Lisa had claimed. They'd have to talk.

Her heart sinking through the floor even though, unselfishly, she was happy for Jamie, Sherry stared at him. "Now?" she asked.

He shook his head. "I vote we let the dust settle ... take a few days to think things over. What would you say to going on a long walk with me at Hillsborough River State Park Saturday afternoon? You could bring Jamie in his stroller. It's usually peaceful out there though there are always a few picnickers and kids rafting. We could hash out the details of what's to be done then."

It didn't sound as if those details were cast in concrete. Or destined to be wrested completely from her hands. "That sounds like a fair proposal," she answered. "We can be ready whenever you want."

He picked them up around 3:00 p.m., his demeanor gentle, his manner toward Jamie full of wonder and affection. The deep bronze of his skin glowing in contrast to his white shorts and Florida Panthers T-shirt. God, but he's a beautiful man. If only I'd met him first, Sherry thought helplessly as he ushered them into the car, dropping an offhand kiss on Jamie's head before putting up the top so the baby wouldn't get sunburned.

The used stroller Sherry had purchased for a couple of bucks at a local garage sale didn't always cooperate when she tried to set it up. But she needn't have worried that she'd have to struggle with it that afternoon. Mike had taken care of things before she'd unbuckled Jamie from his car seat. Moments later, they were headed down a winding, unpaved footpath beneath moss-draped oaks, for all the world like a typical young married couple on a Saturday afternoon outing with their baby.

They were anything but that, no matter how much Sherry wished it otherwise. It broke her heart to think that the precious little boy crowing enthusiastically at a squirrel that scampered in front of them might soon be removed from her care. At least there'll be no sword dangling symbolically over his head, she thought. I'll give him up without a fight rather than do anything to hurt him.

Since Mike held all the aces, she'd let him play the first card. He waited until they'd reached the riverbank and turned to follow its course, brushing aside the low-hanging palm fronds that impeded their progress as they watched the stream's tannin-bronzed water gurgle over mossy wet rocks.

"I've been giving the matter of what to do about Jamie a great deal of thought," he admitted finally, not quite meeting her eyes.

She bent to brush a dragonfly away from the baby's forehead. "So have I," she murmured, sick with anticipation over what might follow.

"It's an area where I don't have much experience," he added. "Legally or paternally. Just getting used to the idea that I have a son has taken some stretching."

About to chastise him mentally for his ambivalence, Sherry opted for lenience instead. In the beginning, she'd had mixed emotions about taking responsibility for her sister's little boy despite the fact that she'd loved him from the moment of his birth. For Mike, becoming a parent had been a lot more precipitous. He was already fond of Jamie. It didn't take an enormous leap of faith to believe that the kind of love she felt for the baby soon would knit him and Jamie together. As her thoughts tumbled through her head in concert with the stream below, she realized something. She'd accepted Mike's stated unawareness that he and Lisa had conceived a child—in effect, taking his word against her sister's. Oddly enough, it wasn't because she cared for him. Even the possibility that he'd take Jamie and refuse her partial custody or visitation didn't seem to make a dent.

It was just that she found him more believable. Fond as she'd been of Lisa too, she was well aware the lovely, captivating blonde had possessed scant regard for the truth. I don't see how she could have fooled around on Mike if she loved him the way she claimed, she thought. I wonder if he loved her, and would have asked her to marry him if she'd told him she was pregnant.

For his part, Mike could sense Sherry's vulnerability. He knew she feared losing Jamie completely, and understood how much she loved the baby. In his opinion, she was a wonderful mother to him. He longed to reassure her, tell her everything would be okay. Yet he wanted a strong hand and definitive role in raising the boy. He was somewhat reluctant to voice the tentative solution he'd worked out because it was such a radical one. In any event, he had serious doubts she'd go for it.

"Despite the abrupt way in which I learned of our relationship and the comparatively short time I've had to contemplate its ramifications, I find myself eager to play a major part in Jamie's life," he went on at last, resorting to legalese in his attempt to vanquish awkwardness. "Yet I deeply value all the love and care you've lavished on him. I'd like it to continue. . . ."

Sherry's heart leapt. He'd share the baby! "So would I," she answered tremulously, feeling as if a colossal weight had been lifted from her chest.

Briefly searching her face, Mike fixed his gaze on the middle distance. "Any suggestions as to how that might come about?" he asked.

To her, the answer seemed obvious. "We could have joint custody," she said. "I'd have him during the week. He'd go to you on weekends. If problems arose, we'd consult. Trade off holidays and special occasions."

"Just like your average divorced parents." Mike's tone made his aversion clear. "Jamie deserves a better start in life than that, don't you think?"

Faced with his blunt delineation of the problems such an arrangement would pose, Sherry had to agree. "Of course I do," she said. "I just don't see any other way."

They'd reached the rustic, motion-prone suspension footbridge that crossed to the stream's opposite bank. Not answering immediately, Mike pushed Jamie's stroller up its weathered planks, pausing to lean against the railing.

"I remember coming out here as a kid and squealing with delight when my dad made this bridge rock by bouncing on it," he said after a moment. "My brother, Joe, my sisters and I used to play ball with him while Mom read one of her novels and set out the picnic lunch. I have a lot of fond memories of this place."

Ostensibly random, his musings made a telling point. He wanted his son to have the kind of family that had nurtured him. As an orphan raised by an elderly, opinionated grandmother who'd worked long hours as a nurse's aide, Sherry had never known that kind of secure existence. But she envied it. She didn't see how it was possible in Jamie's situation. Perhaps wisely, she kept her mouth shut and waited to see what he'd suggest.

"What would you say if I told you I've come up with a plan that would take everyone's rights into account and give Jamie the kind of life we both want for him?" he asked after a long pause in which he'd tried to calculate Sherry's feelings and failed. "Would you be interested . . . even if it called for some sacrifice on your part?"

"Ga-ga-ga!" Jamie interjected, straining to seize a butterfly that hovered briefly within his grasp.

"Butterfly," she said, automatically naming the colorful insect for Jamie's edification. The sun was in her eyes and she reached for her dark glasses. "I suppose I would," she averred.

"Then perhaps you'd agree to marry me."

A bolt from the blue, his proposal left her speechless. Had she heard him correctly? Reason argued in the affirmative. Even as she questioned her sanity, she could feel ecstasy leap. To keep Jamie and have Mike for her husband! No other set of circumstances would have pleased her soul as much.

Hard on the heels of happiness, reality brought a bitter taste. Sure, Mike wanted to go to bed with her, the way he had with other women, including her own sister. But he didn't love her. He was proposing a marriage of convenience for Jamie's sake. He wanted the only mother his sweet baby had known to go on raising him. In the bargain, he'd get live-in help.

Probing her reaction, Mike realized with a twist of discouragement that, at best, it was mixed. She wanted to keep mothering Jamie and she'd been afraid he wouldn't let her. That much was clear, in light of the relief and joy that had washed over her face. Marriage to him, apparently, was another story. Though nothing could make him believe the physical attraction he felt wasn't reciprocated, he had to concede that, for her, *sacrifice* was probably the appropriate word.

Whatever the case, he'd stand by his offer.

"So," he said, concealing the keen discomfort he felt. "What do you think?"

If she answered truthfully, the bargain he was suggesting would be impossible. Love and convenience didn't mix. "Such an option never occurred to me," she said. "I . . . haven't had time to digest it yet."

"Take all the time you want."

They spent a few more minutes on the bridge, commenting on some rafters who were drifting downstream and speaking of the likelihood Jamie would attempt to escape from his stroller soon. Finally, he suggested they should go. "You'll be able to think things over more effectively in private," he submitted. "Just so you know, I envision a union in which each of us could expect the other's financial support... together with the usual conjugal rights."

Unprepared for his statement, Sherry could feel her face flame. As they got in the car and headed back to town, she attempted to make sense of it. Maybe he considers himself too ethical to cheat once he's a married man, but doesn't want to give up sex, she thought. Considering his track record, his scruples might not last long. I'm not sure I could stand it if he was unfaithful.

Thanks to the way she felt about him, she knew she wouldn't be able to lie in his bed night after night and not succumb. What'll I do? she tormented herself. If I say yes, it'll be hard. I'll never be able to forget he married me solely for Jamie's sake, no matter how affectionately I'm treated. On the other hand, too many generations of Hayes and Tompkins children had grown up without two parents. Or even one. She didn't want that for her nephew.

As they sped south on 50th Street from Fowler Avenue, an important truth emerged. She couldn't do without Mike *or* Jamie any longer. Essentially, she didn't have a choice.

Her announcement came as Mike braked for a stoplight. "I've thought it over," she said, turning to him. "And I agree with a lot of what you said. If you were serious, and not just talking, I'll marry you."

Chapter Eight

Convinced as they'd left the park that she'd turn him down, Mike stared at her in disbelief. Did she mean it? Or was she merely testing him? In the seconds that followed, the light turned green. He didn't move. Behind them, someone began to honk. Another driver quickly followed suit.

"I'm serious about this," Mike said, his foot still poised on the brake. "Are you?"

Sherry nodded as the driver of a pickup truck joined in the chorus. "Don't you think we ought to get moving before we have a rebellion on our hands?" she suggested.

Giving her a speaking look, he gunned the Mustang's engine and they took off like a shot. The light was green as they reached Hillsborough Avenue. Abruptly they turned right, heading west. "Where are we going?" Sherry asked.

"To tell my parents."

A little spasm of panic seized her. Had she made the right choice? Once the senior Ruizes knew of their plans, backing out would be sticky. "Must we do it today?" she asked.

"Shouldn't we give ourselves some time . . . get used to the idea first?"

A muscle tightened in Mike's jaw. "Either you're willing to marry me, or you're not," he said. "It's that simple."

So that's how he's going to play it, Sherry thought. He won't settle for anything less than a one hundred percent commitment. "I'm willing," she answered with deceptive calm, considering the fact that her words constituted a personal watershed. "But . . . do they have to know you're Jamie's father?"

His gaze flicked in her direction before refocusing on the other drivers. "You mean now? Or *ever?*"

"It seems to me the news that they're getting another daughter-in-law is enough of a bombshell for one visit."

Mike contemplated her point of view. "I think they have a right to know Jamie's their grandson," he said after a moment. "And I plan to tell them, with or without your say-so. I'll hold off for the time being if it would make you more comfortable."

When his parents find out the truth, they'll guess the reason for our marriage, Sherry thought. I'll have to smile and pretend it doesn't matter . . . that everything turned out okay. Meanwhile, it was beginning to sound as if the ceremony would be rushed. She supposed that, since theirs would be an "arranged marriage" for Jamie's sake, he wanted to get it over with and concentrate on more important business.

Running a comb through her hair and freshening her lipstick with the aid of the flip-down mirror on the Mustang's passenger side, she reflected that, when she'd left her grandmother's house several hours earlier, she'd hadn't bargained on a proposal of marriage from Mike. Or meeting his parents again in the role of a prospective daughter-in-law. In the interim, her life had lurched onto a completely different path than she'd expected it to take.

The remainder of their drive to the Ruizes' neat West Tampa home took place in silence except for Jamie's contented babbling and her occasional remarks to him. In the absence of any conversation with Mike, her rational self started noticing things. He's making statements while you're limiting yourself to asking questions, it observed. That puts him in the driver's seat, figuratively as well as literally. If you want to retain something of your hard-won independence, you'll have to stand up for yourself.

Surprised to see them, Mike's parents were warmly welcoming. "Hi, sweetheart. What a good boy you are!" his mom greeted Jamie after giving her own son a hug. "It's good to see you, Sherry. We were just sitting down to an early supper. Won't you join us? It's *ropa vieja* . . . Mike's favorite."

Mike glanced from her to his father. "Sherry and I have some news for you, Mom and Dad," he said. "Maybe we'd better talk first."

Isabel and Manolo Ruiz exchanged a look. "Of course, son," Manny Ruiz said, tugging at his salt-and-pepper mustache. "Why don't we go into the living room?"

For Sherry, entering the Ruizes' modest living room was like stepping onto a stage set designed to illustrate the kind of family life she'd always envisioned and sorely missed. Though Sandra's wedding had marked the departure of the last sibling from the household, memories of the Ruiz children's idyllic childhood were everywhere she looked.

Photographs told the story. Collected from the time they were babies, dozens of studio portraits and enlarged, framed snapshots of Joe, Mike, Sandra and Kelly Ruiz Castro, the married sister who lived in California, adorned the walls, the bookshelves, the top of the upright piano. The most recent, taken at Sandra's wedding, occupied a place of honor atop the television set.

Many of the photographs showed Manny and Isabel smiling proudly with one or more of their offspring at

Christmas, Easter, the Fourth of July, various birthdays, someone's graduation. Others focused lovingly on their grandchildren—Kelly's twins, Joe's and Kathy's youngsters. One of Mike as a frosting-smeared two-year-old, blowing out birthday candles and looking for all the world like a slightly older version of Jamie, tugged at Sherry's heartstrings.

The family collection also included a formal black-and-white wedding portrait of Isabel and Manny and several fading sepia prints of grandparents and great-grandparents who'd come to the U.S. from Cuba as immigrants. *Jamie's history, his connections are in this room,* Sherry thought, suppressing a shiver of emotion as she sat beside Mike on the couch with the baby on her lap. *I'm glad he's coming home to them.*

"So... what do you want to talk about?" Mike's father asked, leaning forward in his favorite rocker as his wife waited with obvious curiosity, smoothing her apron.

Mike wasn't the sort to mince words. "Sherry and I have decided to get married," he revealed. "I know it's sudden, but..."

"Son, that's wonderful!" Tears of happiness glistening in her eyes, Isabel Ruiz crossed the space between them and tugged them to their feet. A second later, Manny had put his arms around them. Sherry, Mike and Jamie were caught in a two-way crush.

"When's the happy day?" Manny asked, his voice gruff with pleasure as he slapped Mike on the back.

Mike's swift glance told Sherry he'd field the question. "I'm not sure," he murmured. "We just got engaged an hour ago."

Isabel Ruiz was smiling fondly. "We'll have to call Father Tomás," she mused. "Reserve the church. Plan for a reception. We'll help, of course, since Sherry's grandmother can't do it. Too bad you and Sandy couldn't have doubled up..."

"It isn't going to be that kind of wedding, Mom."

Both parents' faces registered astonishment. "You're not getting married in the church?" Isabel asked with a frown. "Mikey... I don't understand."

Having blurted out the first response that came to mind, Mike tried to backtrack from his hard-sounding position without telling them the news Sherry had begged him to keep private for the time being. An embarrassed by-stander, she wanted to curl up inside herself. He'd decided how things would go—without consulting her. Apparently the "how" of their marriage didn't matter, since they weren't entering into it for their sakes, just Jamie's. Re-treating behind a wall of silence, she felt nothing so much as relief when he begged off from the meal they'd been in-vited to share with the excuse that Sherry had several tasks to perform in advance of her grandmother's homecoming from the hospital, which would take place the following afternoon.

I don't want to back out of my promise to him, she thought a short time later as he parked outside Lillian Hayes's frame cottage and walked them to the door. Just to be treated like my needs matter. And to be loved. Un-fortunately, neither of those prizes were likely to be hers. For the time being, it would have to be enough that he loved and wanted Jamie.

Sensing her unhappiness, Mike tried clumsily to set things straight. "Look," he said. "I took the ball and ran with it at my parents' house. If you want a church wed-ding..."

The way things had turned out between them, it would be a charade. She shook her head. "Holding the ceremony at your church rectory will be fine," she answered. "I'm just a little stunned at everything that's happened, I guess."

He could relate to that. "Okay, then," he said after a moment. "If you're sure."

"I am. Under the circumstances, it'd probably be best."

I wonder how I'd feel if things were different between us, and we were marrying out of love, not just so we could both keep Jamie, Mike thought as he dropped a light kiss on her cheek and headed for his car. I'd probably be one deliriously happy guy. Instead I'm brusque, emotionally distant. I just don't know any other way of dealing with this.

Morning came and with it, for Sherry, renewed hope. In the wee hours, restless with lack of sleep, she'd convinced herself a better outcome might lie in store. If she exercised a modicum of patience and shared Mike's bed the way he wanted to, love might grow. He might come to care for her the way he'd apparently cared for Lisa before her infidelity had prompted him to break off their relationship.

Her grandmother's mostly negative reaction to Sherry's plans spoiled her confidence only a little. She couldn't help flinching, though, at the older woman's comment that at least she'd gotten the *promise* of a ring on her finger.

"I gather you ain't offered Mike Ruiz milk before he bought the cow, the way Lisa did," Lillian Hayes chuckled somewhat offensively as Sherry made her comfortable in her favorite chair.

No, I haven't. And I don't intend to, Sherry retorted silently as she plumped the older woman's pillow. It's bad enough that we fell in love with the same man. Their affair will always haunt me.

The rest of Sunday passed in relative quiet if not tranquillity with Sherry taking her promised phone call from Mike, caring for Jamie and making a quick trip to the mall with the latter in tow to search for a wedding outfit. During their brief phone conversation, Mike had suggested they tie the knot the following weekend and she'd seen no reason to object. Despite the arranged quality of their marriage, it would be a relief to get out from under her grandmother's roof, she realized as she thumbed through a rack of marked-down dressmaker suits that remained too pricey for her budget.

If only she could find an affordable outfit—something that would transform her from Lisa's younger sister and Jamie's stand-in mom into a vision of radiance and allure that would sweep Mike off his feet. . . .

"Looking for something special, miss?" a middle-aged store clerk asked.

Sherry hesitated. "I realize these suits are a bargain," she acknowledged, "but they're still beyond my price range. I'm getting married next Saturday..."

Clearly an outspoken type, the salesclerk dared to ask the obvious question. "To your baby's father, dear?"

Despite her innocence in the matter of Jamie's conception, Sherry blushed.

The woman gave her a conspiratorial smile. "We may have just the ticket, hon. You're about a size eight, aren't you? If you can sew..."

From a backroom rack of damaged garments, the salesclerk brought forth a luminous silk twill fitted suit in a ravishing shade of aqua that would compliment Sherry's complexion. As is, the former top-of-the-line offering could be had for fifty dollars. Though several of its seams were split and most of its buttons hung by a thread, Sherry could see at once that it was essentially in good shape.

As she tried it on before one of the dressing room mirrors while Jamie played peekaboo behind her thigh, she could imagine herself wearing it in one of the Ruiz family's living room portraits. I may be a crazy optimist, she thought as she pirouetted to regard herself in profile, but I can't help believing things will work out. The way I love him and Jamie, they just *have* to. I'll simply banish all contrary thoughts.

Doubt had regained the ascendancy by the following Saturday as she dressed for the ceremony that would unite her and Mike in marriage at the residence of the Ruizes' parish priest. Am I doing the right thing? she wondered for perhaps the thousandth time, fretting over the possibility that Mike had neglected to buy her a ring. Or will I have regrets? In her book, marriage was forever once the vows were said.

It didn't help that, shortly before quitting time the previous afternoon, Mike had taken her aside to inform her he'd told his parents about Jamie.

"What...did they say?" she'd stammered, concerned their reaction might overshadow the following day's event.

Mike had *shrugged*. "They were awfully surprised," he'd admitted. "Maybe *shocked* would be a better word. Mom's thrilled, of course, despite some confusion on her part. She thinks the world of Jamie. And she'll never have enough grandchildren. Dad just listened to my explanation, and didn't say much."

If the Ruizes developed qualms about whether their son was marrying her for the right reasons, she doubted they'd express them to her. Meanwhile, their reservations wouldn't be the only ones. I have a bunch of my own, and so does Mike, despite his cool, take-charge attitude, she wagered as she buttoned her refurbished suit jacket and dabbed a little extra perfume behind her ears. Her grandmother certainly had made no bones about what she thought would be the outcome.

In Lillian Hayes's opinion, Mike and Sherry would be divorced within a year. "What do you care, gal?" she'd asked in response to Sherry's pained look. "You're just doin' this for Jamie's sake, ain't you? The way I see it, you'll get both child support *and* alimony."

As Sherry and her dark-haired fiancé had arranged, his older brother, Joe, who would serve as his best man, arrived around 2:00 p.m. to drive Sherry, her grandmother and Jamie to the rectory. Meanwhile, at Mike's West Shore apartment, Hector was removing the groom's boutonniere from a cardboard florist's box. The nosegay of white roses and baby's breath Mike's mother had insisted he order for Sherry lay beside it in a box of its own on his heavy oak dresser.

"Sure you know what you're doing, *amigo?*" Mike's deputy director asked as he handed over the taped carnation.

"Yeah." His expression prohibiting further discourse on the subject, Mike arranged the posy in the lapel of his lawyerly pin-striped suit.

Hector had never been one to take a hint. "Why don't you look happier, then?" he persisted.

"Maybe I've got a lot on my mind."

Uneasy about what would transpire between him and Sherry when they were alone that evening, and irate at having his uncertainties articulated against his will, Mike decided to silence his friend once and for all. "There's something you don't know," he added. "You remember Lisa Hayes...the blonde I dated for a while? Well, Sherry's her sister. The baby you think of as her son is really Lisa's."

Hector stared at him in disbelief. "You're kidding, man."

Mike shook his head. "To complicate things even more, I'm Jamie's father, though I didn't realize it until just a few days ago. Put that in your pipe and smoke it."

Reached at her honeymoon hideaway two days before she and her husband were scheduled to return home, Sandra had agreed to stand up for Sherry and her brother. She'd received the news about Jamie's parentage from her mother by phone, as well. Now, ushered into the rectory's neat, old-fashioned parlor by the parish housekeeper just moments after Joe had deposited Sherry, Jamie and Sherry's grandmother there, Sandra greeted the bride-to-be with an effusive hug.

"How wonderful to have you and Jamie in the family," she exclaimed, bussing Sherry affectionately on the cheek, as her mother temporarily took charge of the baby. "I couldn't be happier."

Does she *know?* Sherry wondered. "I suppose someone . . . Mike or your mom . . . has told you that Jamie's really Mike's son," she answered, her smile a little forced.

"His and your late sister's. Yes, I know about it. In my opinion, it only makes your getting together more marvelous."

For some reason, apparently, Sandra seemed to think Mike was marrying for love instead of making the best of a tangled situation. I'll believe it when I hear it from him, Sherry thought as Mike arrived and greeted her with a light kiss.

Gazing down at her, Mike thought how lovely and uncertain she looked. In her beautiful aqua suit, with the tawny strands in her silky brown hair catching the light, she was a bride any man would be proud to claim. It's possible we'd have come to this joining of the ways without Jamie's needs lighting a fire under us, he reflected. I might have had the good sense to settle down with her anyway.

By now, his shock and anger at being deceived by Sherry's investigation of him had largely dissipated. His desire for her had regained the upper hand. He wanted to fall asleep with the soft mounds of her breasts touching him, invade and ravish her most secret places. Yet they'd barely kissed. He didn't have the slightest idea what, if anything, she felt for him.

Mutually burdened with questions, they turned as the Ruizes' pastor, Father Tomás Beresford, entered the room. After greeting each family member and introducing himself politely to Sherry's grandmother, the priest huddled briefly with them. The special dispensation that would allow them to be married at once without taking the usual prenuptial classes had been granted by the bishop of St.

Petersburg. The wedding was a go from the church's standpoint. Were they ready to begin?

Meeting each other's eyes with full knowledge of the risk they were taking, Mike and Sherry nodded in the affirmative.

"Good." Father Tomás raised his voice slightly. "Dearly beloved, if you'll gather around..."

Later, Sherry wouldn't have been able to repeat the words that were spoken as she and Mike stood before his Cuban-born pastor and recited their marriage vows. She'd simply remember being awarded her heart's desire while—she believed—having it simultaneously dangled beyond her reach. Only the kiss sanctioned by Father Tomás as part of the ceremony would remain forever fresh.

Putting his arms around her as their assembled relatives had watched and waited, Mike had enfolded her so gently that the hand on which he'd unexpectedly slipped his great-grandmother's plain gold wedding band a few minutes earlier rested with the delicacy of a wild bird against his chest. Though his kiss was equally restrained, a public rite of passage that wouldn't cause undue whispering, its latent passion penetrated her defenses like an arrow shot. He'll demand everything and give back nothing of himself, she thought, responding helplessly. I wish to God I didn't love him so much.

For her, the family's postwedding celebration at The Colonnade, a festive, moderately elegant restaurant overlooking Hillsborough Bay, passed in a blur. Numb though she was, she couldn't help being aware of the many whispers and assessing looks that stemmed from Jamie's parentage. Barely touching her filet and sipping only sparingly at the champagne a waiter had poured without asking her, she did her best to smile whenever a toast was made.

She also posed without complaining for an endless variety of pictures with her sister's baby, her husband and various newly acquired relatives. Most of the photographs had captured her holding Jamie, she guessed, though Mike took over the task for several frames. Suffering from an attack of shyness, the little boy she was now free to call her own refused to sit in the high chair that had been provided for him, or to try out his new walking skills when Joe's son, ten-year-old Joe, Jr., offered to take his hand. Always vociferous if he wanted something, Jamie insisted on occupying her lap as a secure haven in a crowd of strangers.

His insistence on clinging to her when Mike announced it was time to go broke her heart. "Grandma Ruiz will take good care of you, sweetheart," she reassured him, reluctantly loosening his baby stranglehold around her neck. "Your playpen's at her house, along with most of your toys, so you won't get bored. Besides...Sherry will be back in the morning."

He didn't understand, of course. How could he? At eleven months, such explanations were miles above his head. His bereft wail followed them into the parking lot, adding a painful dimension to an already awkward moment.

"He'll be all right," Mike reassured, stashing his suit jacket in the Mustang's trunk.

Sherry nodded. "I know. It's just that he's so little. And he doesn't understand."

Should he offer to take the baby with them? Holding the passenger door open for her and then getting behind the wheel, Mike decided against it. For an optimum start on their new life together, they needed to be alone in the Clearwater Beach motel room he'd reserved for them. Putting down the convertible top in order to enjoy the breeze since Jamie wouldn't be a passenger, he started the engine and headed out of the parking lot.

Conversation was almost nonexistent during their drive to the beach. Her hair blowing wildly as they crossed the bay and raced past one yellow light after another on their way through Clearwater, Sherry wondered what lay ahead.

It wasn't that she doubted Mike meant to make love to her. On the day he'd proposed, he'd made it abundantly clear that he would. They hadn't left Jamie behind so they could stroll down the beach unencumbered.

It was just that she felt so inexperienced, so conscious of the fact he wouldn't have married her at all if it hadn't been for her sister's baby and the question of who would raise him. A complete novice at sex who knew herself to be desired but doubted that she'd ever be loved, she couldn't seem to stop wondering how she'd stack up against the women who figured in Mike's past—in particular, against her half sister. Though she did her best to banish the picture from her head, she found it painfully easy to imagine her egregious sibling in his arms.

She'd never been able to understand why Lisa hadn't told him about the baby. Now that she'd heard his version of what had split them up, she was willing to bet she knew the reason. In her opinion, Lisa had kept silent out of vanity. She'd have been forced to eat crow—and face justifiable doubts about her baby's parentage—if she'd asked Mike for child support after cheating on him.

It's anybody's guess whether she'd understand what we're trying to do and wish us well, or mock me for falling in love with him, Sherry thought. One thing's certain, though. She'd be pleased as heck to know Mike's still sufficiently invested in her to feel the sting of a two-year-old betrayal.

The motel he'd chosen for their wedding night was situated directly on the beach, a short distance north of the bridge and palm-studded causeway that spanned the intracoastal waterway. As they arrived, the sun was edging toward the horizon, suffusing the sky with its ruddy glory.

Finger-combing the tangles from her hair, Sherry waited in the car while Mike registered. He was back in a moment with the key, ready to move the Mustang to an overnight parking space. "I was able to get us a room facing the water," he remarked as they parked and put up the convertible top. "We should have a good vantage point to watch the sunset."

They would if they hurried. Clutching her overnight bag as if it were a security blanket, Sherry preceded him up the steps. The room he'd reserved contained the usual TV, desk-and-dresser combination plus a king-size bed with a peach-and-tan geometric print cover that seemed to dominate everything. As she paused to stare at it with parted lips, Mike swept back the drapes and unlocked the glass slider.

She isn't making this any easier, he thought, stepping out onto their private balcony. "Come out and join me," he invited, careful not to sound as if he were pressuring her.

Placing her overnight bag on a chair, Sherry did as he asked. Though he tugged her against his side with one arm about her waist, he didn't try to kiss her or unbutton her jacket. Instead, he continued to gaze at some sailboarders who were packing up and a cruise ship headed for port.

How good his after-shave smells...like rain and musk laced with exotic spices, Sherry thought. But it's his unadorned skin scent I like best. With everything that was erotic and womanly in her, she longed to nestle closer still, bury her face against his shirt.

Their nuptial night, with its misgivings and untapped glory, would come just once in the sequence of twenty-seven thousand or so she could expect. Would she be able to forget his liaison with her sister, set the reasons for their marriage aside and avail herself of its bounty? Spreading on the sand below like cast nets fashioned of lace, an endless succession of breakers seemed to answer *yes*.

By now, the sun had flattened to an ovoid copper disk. Soon it would appear to slip beneath the waters of the Gulf of Mexico. Pleasantly cool if a little humid, the Florida night would draw them into its embrace.

Let it happen, Mike begged without words, his fingers lightly stroking her sleeve. Open yourself to the pleasure we can know together. In ways I don't begin to understand, you and I were meant. The very last thing he wanted was to coerce her, make love if that wasn't what she felt.

Somehow, she caught the tenor of his thoughts, though not their specificity. It was enough to abolish her fears. Turning toward him with a full heart the way she'd longed to do from the very first, she slipped her arms around his neck.

"Ah, Sherry..."

His smothered outcry rough-edged with longing, Mike took complete possession of her mouth. In an instant, she was spiraling beyond her depth. Though they'd kissed before, no previous joining of their lips had served as an open door to paradise. *This* one would. It quickly proved its potency. His tongue fusing their separateness, he made her moist privacy his with a forthright boldness that left little doubt of what they'd do together.

Her nipples tightening at the prospect, Sherry swayed a little as he slid one hand up her thigh, beneath her skirt. Did he plan to take her there on the balcony with her legs wrapped around his waist?

"Mike, please," she remonstrated. "Not here."

"You're right. We don't want to create a spectacle."

Sweeping her up in arms so strong she couldn't imagine their equal, he carried her inside, to the bed. Before she realized how it had come about, his shirt lay crumpled on the floor beside his shoes and her skirt was pushed up about her waist. He'd separated her jacket buttons from their buttonholes. Moments later, the front clasp of her bra had yielded to his hunger. His lean, tanned fingers expertly grappling with the fasteners of her garter belt as her breasts spilled free, he took one rosy, upturned peak in his mouth.

Caught in a firestorm of sensation, Sherry thought she'd burn to ashes with wanting him. Hungry as a spark consuming a lighted fuse, arousal sped to the depths he'd be the first to claim. Seconds later, her incandescence had doubled in intensity. His thumb teasing her other nipple into taut submission, Mike thrust a knee between her legs. Raising his head to look at her, he lowered it again to kiss her eyes, her mouth, her neck.

"Yes...oh, yes," she moaned. "Mike...I want you."

"Let me do this for you first."

At some point, he'd removed her nylon stockings and skirt. Now, with a facility that whispered of his experience with other women, he took off her panties as well. Damp, vulnerable, a flower in first bloom, she lay exposed to his gaze, his touch.

"You're so beautiful..." The accolade muffled against her nest of golden-brown curls, he burrowed deeper, to pay homage with his tongue.

Precipitously, the longing he'd evoked concentrated at a point of white-hot intensity. Helplessness flooded her. Clutching at his thick, dark hair to anchor herself, she let sensation take her. Up and up it lifted her, into a spiral of pleasure that knew no bounds. Abruptly she passed a point of no return. Her bare feet gripping the bed for purchase, she dissolved in a paroxysm of shudders that released a sea of warmth throughout her body.

"That's it, baby," Mike murmured approvingly. "Take it as far as it can go."

Gradually, she stilled, every muscle quiescent, and began to drift. Mike had given her such magnificence. And taken nothing for himself.

What he'd done wasn't half of what they could do together. She knew that much. "Mike, you haven't..." she protested.

"I will, *mi esposa,* I promise you."

Removing his lawyer's pin-striped trousers and the boxer shorts he wore beneath them, he repositioned himself between her legs. After weeks of fantasizing, he'd have her. He was hot and ready. In the hope of taking her with him, he inserted his finger first, and met with unexpected resistance.

The little cry of pain she couldn't stifle cut him to the quick. "Sherry...sweetheart." His voice was troubled. "Tell me I haven't hurt you."

"You haven't. Oh, you haven't. Mike, it's just that..." Concerned and heavy with wanting her, he waited.

"I'm a virgin."

It was as if she'd administered an electrical shock. Or poured a pitcher of ice water over him. "You've got to be kidding!" he exclaimed.

From the vantage point of his experience, Mike seemed to view her untouched state as a detriment. "I'm sorry, but it's true," she confessed.

Stunned, he didn't know what to do. "Tell me why you married me," he said after a moment.

Her surrender to him complete as she lay there naked in his arms, Sherry felt suddenly as if she must defend herself. "The same reason you married me," she responded, stating what had been a half truth from the beginning. "Two parents for Jamie."

God help him. It was as he'd feared. She'd agreed to sacrifice the treasure she'd guarded on the altar of a baby's need, and now she'd keep her word. Like some lout who bore no resemblance to the person he'd believed himself to be, he hadn't bothered to ask if the physical side of marriage to him was something she could accept. He'd simply assumed the sexual attraction he felt was mutual, and handed down terms.

Giving her a look that broke her heart and caused her to cover herself with one corner of the bedspread in embarrassment, he got up and retrieved his shorts.

"I can't let you make that kind of sacrifice," he said without expression.

Chapter Nine

It was dusk—dark enough for casual strollers on the beach to see into the room if anyone inside it approached the windows. With Mike absent, walking to clear his head, Sherry peeled back the bedspread she'd wrapped about herself and shut the balcony drapes before switching on her bedside lamp and putting on her nightgown. Mechanically she hung up the rumpled silk suit she'd refurbished with such high hopes.

I can't go home to Gram or show up on the Ruizes' doorstep demanding Jamie, she realized, stifling an urge to flee. Even if I could catch a bus back to Tampa, pick up my car and confront Mike's parents before he caught up with me, I'd no longer have a home where I could take a baby. Or a job to support him. All too well, she knew the kind of behavior she was contemplating would spawn an aggressive custody suit.

Unable to staunch the tears that kept welling up over the debacle their wedding night had become, she got back into bed, pulled the covers up to her chin and punched the lamp's On-Off button. The latter move threw the room into almost total darkness. Only the bathroom light, which cast a narrow ribbon of illumination over the closet area from behind a partially closed door, greeted Mike on his return.

"Sher...you awake?" he asked softly, kicking off the shoes he'd worn sockless on the sand and removing his slacks and shirt.

Though she'd heard his key turn in the lock, Sherry didn't answer him. Curled up on the far side of the bed, with her back turned and her breathing smooth and regular, she appeared to be fast asleep.

He didn't quite believe it.

Alone on the beach, as he'd strode and thought, he'd undergone a partial change of heart. The fact of Sherry's virginity didn't mean, ipso facto, that she didn't want to have sex with him. In truth, her *behavior* had argued to the contrary. Though she'd been shy, she'd also been passionate. Now that she'd decided to rebuff any attempt on his part to resolve things by pretending sleep, he wasn't quite sure what to do.

"Sher?" he asked again.

There wasn't any answer. Switching off the bathroom light, he got into bed in his shorts though he usually slept nude. A slender ridge beneath the blanket on the opposite side of the king-size bed, Sherry seemed miles away. In practical terms, he supposed, she might as well have been on another planet. Silently cursing the mess he'd made of things, Mike shut his eyes. It was a long time before he fell asleep.

When the phone rang early the next morning, he was dreaming. "Hello?" he answered groggily, having noted Sherry's absence as he'd fumbled for the receiver.

The caller was Hector. "I know it's your honeymoon, man," his second-in-command said apologetically. "But you told me to phone if Nat Harris needed to get in touch..."

Nat Harris was a powerful state senator who'd lent his support to the migrant-rights bill Mike had been working so hard to pass. If a crucial committee meeting had been moved up...or the bill had hit a snag... He shrugged. There was no telling. Rubbing the sleep from his eyes, he dialed the legislator's private number and hoped for the best.

A short time later, he located Sherry on the beach and called out her name. Without so much as an answering hello or a wave, she paused and waited for him to catch up to her. Though her demeanor lacked sparkle, she looked pretty and clean-scrubbed in her yellow shorts and T-shirt. Only a faint smudginess beneath her eyes hinted at a restless night.

Briefly the words, *Sorry about what happened. Let's try again,* hovered on his lips. He couldn't subdue his pride sufficiently to articulate them. "Hector just phoned," he told her instead. "I've got to drive up to Tallahassee right away. The bill I've been shepherding through the legislature just hit a roadblock. Can you pick up Jamie if I give you the key to my apartment and drop you off at your grandmother's to get your car?"

Stubbornly private behind the emotional wall she'd erected for her own protection, Sherry nodded her head.

She hadn't visited Mike's condo before marrying him. Now she lived there. Alone in his contemporary, somewhat impersonal one-bedroom, one-bath unit that evening after unpacking their things and putting Jamie to bed in a small semi-separate study area off the bedroom, she sat on a small, screened-in porch that offered a glimpse of the bay and wondered what the future would hold.

The past presented numerous obstacles of its own. Unless Mike had moved from one condo to another in the same building during the previous year and a half, the place where she and her nephew now resided had been the site of Mike's torrid affair with Lisa and their baby's conception.

During the ninth month of her sister's pregnancy, they'd been driving home past the Bahia Palms complex when Lisa had pointed it out. "That's where we were living when Mike knocked me up, the uncaring bastard," she'd remarked sarcastically, cradling her swollen stomach.

Having come to believe Mike's version of what had taken place, Sherry no longer saw him as the heartless woman-izer her sister had painted. Unfortunately, the metamorphosis in her thinking had opened the door to some very painful speculation. Thanks to the bitterness Mike had displayed when he'd told her about finding Lisa with an-other man, she was convinced he'd genuinely cared for her sister. Face facts...he *loved* her, she told herself now as she listened to a chuck-will's-widow mournfully calling its mate. She was the kind of woman men are crazy about. If she hadn't cheated on him, he might have married her—even if she hadn't gotten pregnant.

Such thoughts, of course, only tended to sharpen the unhappy comparisons she was bound to make. Lisa's pas-sionate trysts with him had mocked her pain when he'd re-fused to consummate their marriage. She'd think of her sister nestled in his arms when it was time to fall asleep in the teak platform bed they'd once shared.

Scheduled to be off work Monday and Tuesday in order to settle into her new home, Sherry drove over to her grandmother's the following morning to pick up a list so she could buy the older woman some groceries. Inevitably Lillian Hayes took the opportunity to offer her latest opin-ion on the subject of Sherry's marriage. "I been thinkin', gal," she'd decreed from her easy chair. "And I'm con-vinced it was a mistake...."

Tempted to agree after an evening spent hoping Mike would call and a second sleepless night in which she'd contemplated filing for an annulment, Sherry longed to beg her to shut her mouth.

In Tallahassee on Tuesday, Mike could barely concentrate. The disaster to his migrant bill averted in a late-running conference, he caught what sleep he could and started for home the following morning around 2:30 a.m. At 7:29 a.m., he was inserting his key in the lock of his condo's front door.

Inside, the stereo was playing something by the Indigo Girls. He could hear the shower running. Waving a graham cracker in one grubby fist, Jamie babbled a welcome from his playpen.

As he kissed his son's sweet head, the shower shut off. Entering the bedroom without knocking, he surprised Sherry drying herself with one of his oversize towels. Naked and flushed from the warm water, with her chin-length hair curling about her face, she looked startled, vulnerable and incredibly beautiful. *What a fool you were not to make love to her,* he reproached himself.

She didn't voice them, but Sherry was entertaining identical thoughts. For a hot moment, she almost believed he'd pull her into his arms. It didn't happen—at least, not quickly enough to keep her from wrapping the towel more securely around herself. "Have you had breakfast yet?" she asked pointedly. "There's coffee and cereal in the kitchen. I'll join you in a moment."

At his dinette table a few minutes later, Mike filled her in on the success of his mission to Tallahassee and passed along some interesting news. According to Hector, with whom he'd conversed by phone the previous evening, the parents of her young friend Armand had turned up. The church that had sponsored the FFU picnic had offered the family temporary quarters. Several of its members were helping the father look for work. Bowled over at being the recipients of so much help, including a promise by Hector that FFU would intercede for them with U.S. immigration officials, Armand's parents had agreed to testify against Brumpton Groves before the Morgan County Commission.

"It's just the break we've been looking for," Mike said. "Unfortunately, by itself, it won't be enough. We need firsthand evidence from someone the commission can't discount. It's time to put my plan into action."

The idea of her handsome, dark-haired husband exposing himself to injury at the hands of an abusive overseer undermined Sherry's composure. "You're talking about going undercover, aren't you?" she asked worriedly. "Won't that be awfully dangerous?"

Her question elicited the first smile Mike had given her since learning she wasn't Jamie's birth mother. He shook his head indulgently.

"Then you won't object to my going with you."

Astonished she'd even consider such a thing, Mike stared. "You've got to be kidding," he said after a moment.

"Actually, I'm dead serious." Amazed at her own audacity, Sherry bit into a piece of toast. If it took extraordinary measures to win him, she'd resort to them. It couldn't be allowed to matter that he'd probably always love Lisa best. "I could interview the women laborers for you," she added. "They might flirt with you. But they'd tell *me* what was bothering them."

Though he could see her point, Mike didn't budge. "You're forgetting that you have a baby to look after," he said.

We have a baby to look after, Sherry told him silently. But she didn't phrase her argument in those terms. "No, I'm not," she disagreed. "When I picked up Jamie on Sunday, your mother offered to watch him whenever we wanted. In her opinion, we ought to get out of town for a few days."

A trip to Brumpton Groves was hardly what his mother had in mind. At the moment, there wasn't time to resolve the issue. Riding with Mike, Sherry dashed into Marta Ramirez's Sunshine Day Care Center long enough to drop off Jamie before accompanying him to the office. Once there, Mike got on the phone and called an emergency board meeting for 1:00 p.m. that afternoon. Despite the last minute nature of his summons, they managed to achieve a quorum. As Sherry took notes, the board members who'd been able to attend were subjected to the full force of Mike's persuasive personality as he pleaded his case.

Though they were reluctant to let him mount an undercover operation against a private grove owner, they finally agreed. "If you're determined to go, we may as well give you our blessing," joked the gray-haired man who'd called him 'Miguelito' at the first board meeting Sherry had transcribed.

"Does that do it?" a heavyset female member asked after an official vote had been taken. "If so, I'd like..."

"There's just one more point." The words were Sherry's. She hadn't spoken as her pen had raced over the lined pages of her stenographer's notebook, and all eyes turned toward her in astonishment. "As you may know, Mike and I were married last weekend," she added matter-of-factly. "I'm very interested in his work and FFU's goals. I'd like the board's permission to go along on his fact-finding mission."

Predictably, her untoward request stirred fresh controversy. To her surprise, though Mike continued to oppose her, Hector supported it. "She'd be a damn good witness for you in front of the Morgan County Commission, Miguelito," her erstwhile critic argued.

Eventually Mike and the board members who shared his opinion gave in against their better judgement. With a wry, I-don't-believe-this-is-happening look on his face, Mike phoned his mother after the board members had left. He and Sherry hoped to go out of town for a few days beginning on Thursday evening, per her suggestion, he said. Could she and Dad baby-sit? If it was inconvenient . . .

Leaving no doubt about the affection she felt for her most recently acquired grandchild, Isabel Ruiz declared herself more than available. She sounded somewhat relieved, in Mike's opinion. With her keen instinct for her children's lives, he guessed, she'd realized something wasn't quite kosher between him and Sherry. Now, she hoped, they were going to settle it.

I hope so too, *mamacita,* he thought as he put down the receiver and advised Sherry her participation was a go. Nothing would please me better. If I sound skeptical about our runaway weekend to a local resort, chalk it up to the fact that I'm a little old-fashioned, like Papa. I don't like my pretty new wife accompanying me to such a place.

Though by now they'd been married four days, Sherry continued to be his wife in name only. Fortunately, despite a lingering awkwardness that prevented them from putting it into words, they seemed to have agreed upon a truce— one that allowed them to pick up Jamie at the workday's end, return to Mike's apartment and share a pizza, sleep on opposite sides of his queen-size bed without too much discomfort.

I feel more like a partner in our upcoming adventure than I do a wife or a secretary, Sherry thought the following morning as they packed up baby paraphernalia and supplies for Jamie's stay with his Ruiz grandparents.

Later, after a typical if somewhat tense morning at the office, they met with Hector to discuss last-minute arrangements and choose appropriate clothing for their mission from the pile of secondhand, typical migrant apparel he'd rounded up for them.

Sherry settled on ragged jeans and a faded shirt. Though she'd cut her nails short and removed their soft rose enamel, she balked at the ill-fitting bra and clean but shapeless panties Mike wanted her to wear. "Is it really necessary to go this far?" she asked.

"I'm afraid so," he answered. "Don't forget . . . you'll need to pass muster at the bathhouse."

In response to Sherry's raised eyebrows, Mike explained the conditions they'd face. Most of the battered trailers and cabins at Brumpton Groves didn't have running water. They'd have to carry any they needed for cooking or drinking from a central pump. Sanitary facilities were limited to outhouses and communal showers separated by corrugated metal partitions.

"Want to change your mind?" he asked.

Though she hadn't realized what she was getting into, Sherry shook her head. "I can stand anything for a couple of days," she insisted.

They stopped for dinner at a franchise steakhouse in Brandon before completing their drive east, to Morgan County, with Hector behind the wheel of his pickup truck. It was dusk as they neared the camp. "Any other instructions, Mikey?" Hector asked.

"Just to bust down the gate if you haven't heard from us in three days."

"You got it. *Buena suerte. Y cuidado.*"

Decelerating slightly, so that he approached the gate like a driver casually dropping off a pair of hitchhikers, Hector bade them farewell.

The gate was locked and, though several movement-sensitive floodlights switched on at their approach, it took them five or six minutes, alternately yelling and leaning on the buzzer that was marked in several languages, Ring for Admittance, before they were able to attract someone. Finally a leathery man in his fifties or early sixties, with thinning hair, a bulbous red nose and the air of drinking too much, sauntered over to see what they wanted.

"Somebody told us you are looking for workers," Mike told him with a heavy Spanish accent.

"Maybe you heard right." The man spat sourly. "You packin' any iron, José? Can your girlfriend work?"

Though a muscle twitched beside Mike's mouth at having a generic Spanish name assigned to him, he answered respectfully. "*No tengo pistola, señor.* My wife is willing."

Shrugging, the man opened the gate. "Don't tell Curly that if you don't want him chasin' her," he said.

Following the man, who introduced himself as Ralph, the camp payroll clerk and bookkeeper, to the porch of a shabby building that housed his office, they met two additional Brumpton employees, who were smoking on the steps. Curly, the labor boss, a sneering, sinewy man in his twenties with greasy, light-colored hair and a Colt .45 tucked into his belt, and Jolene, a forty-something bottle redhead who ran the adjacent store and canteen, regarded them as if they were beneath contempt. As if it involved no contradiction for him, Curly looked Sherry up and down as if she had a For Sale sign around her neck.

"Names?" Ralph asked, shrugging off Curly's lewdness as he retrieved a somewhat crumpled form. "Where's your car? How come you don't have no suitcases?"

Courteously Mike introduced them as Miguel and Sherry Flores of Immokalee. He explained that their ancient pickup truck had broken down several months ago. Lacking the money for repairs, they'd had to abandon it. At their last stop in east Hillsborough, somebody had stolen their luggage.

Ralph appeared to accept their story. As Sherry listened to his recitation of the camp rules—work hours from 6:00 a.m. to 6:00 p.m., curfew at 7:00 p.m., no purchase of food, beverages or cigarettes except on the premises, docked wages for fighting or insubordination—Sherry thought Brumpton Groves sounded more like prison than a voluntary labor site. Despite her knowledge that they'd be there just a few days, his demand that they pay a week's rent in advance and deposit the balance of their cash in the store safe "on account" for future purchases left Sherry feeling more powerless than she had in a lifetime not noted for its financial security or options.

A group of young men, one of whom wore a rosary around his neck, sauntered up to buy beer and Jolene went inside to accommodate them. Meanwhile, Ralph ushered her and Mike into the office, where Mike was frisked for weapons and signed some papers. When the formalities had been completed, Ralph led them back outside and pointed at a weed-choked field littered with old cars, trailers and run-down cabins. They'd find the mobile home assigned to them in the last row. Nobody else was living in it at the moment.

"That's why I had to charge you the full one hundred sixty dollars," he told them with a gap-toothed smirk as Curly, who was still lounging and smoking, looked down the front of Sherry's shirt.

"I'll borrow a bucket from somebody and get us some drinking water," Mike said after the two men had gone back inside to watch wrestling on Ralph's portable television.

Reluctant to be parted from him, even for a minute, Sherry didn't release his hand. From some of the trailers and cabins, which spilled yellow light, Hispanic music was playing on the radio. A dog barked and then whined as someone cuffed it. Somewhere, a woman laughed. She caught the wail of a child, men swearing over a card game. Here and there, a firefly stab at the dark identified a smoker.

"Okay with you?" Mike prodded.

For some reason—the poverty of her early years, perhaps—handing over their money had made her fear starvation. She was determined to buy them something to eat.

"I'll just run to the store and pick up a few things," she volunteered.

Mike raised his brows. "That should be an education."

In the store, where Jolene had settled down with a back copy of *People* magazine following her customers' departure, Sherry purchased a loaf of white bread and some peanut butter—signing for a deduction from their deposit and secretly gasping at the cost. As she put down the pen, which was tied by a string to Jolene's ancient adding machine, the storekeeper gave her a derisive look.

"Them's mighty soft hands you got," the woman said. "By tomorrow night, they're gonna be covered with blisters from pickin'. Serves you right for takin' up with a wetback."

Jolene's prejudiced characterization of Mike caused Sherry to do a slow burn. Though she didn't answer back, the anger it generated filled her with enough spunk to make it to their trailer on her own. Once she saw its condition, however, she burst into tears. "We can't sleep here!" she exclaimed.

I was afraid of this, Mike thought. "It'll be all right, Sher . . . I promise," he said, holding out his arms.

Chapter Ten

Though they didn't make love as they lay together beneath the rough blanket that was their bed's only covering, Sherry's head was pillowed on Mike's shoulder. Curled on her side, she was snuggled up against him. I wonder if we'll ever consummate our marriage, she thought, her eyelids drifting shut despite her contention just a short time earlier that sleep would be impossible in such a setting. Other men have found me attractive. Surely I'm woman enough to tempt him.

Morning and the grim reality of life at Brumpton Groves arrived in a dizzying rush. The humid, velvety dark that had cradled them erupted with babies crying to be fed, the din of rock and *mariachi* music emanating from a half dozen radios, pots rattling, people arguing and calling to each other in accents that had originated in such diverse places as Haiti, Appalachia and Mexico.

Stirring, Mike dug into the pocket of his jeans for the watch he'd taken off and hidden there as they'd approached the gate. According to its luminous dial, it was

5:21 a.m. Sherry's soft, even breathing barely fluttering against the tangle of dark hair that covered his chest, his wife of five days was still fast asleep.

Gently he shook her awake. "Time to get dressed, *querida*," he said.

Lost in a confusing dream that involved her, Mike, Jamie and her dead sister, Sherry had been sleeping too soundly to catch the endearment. Somehow, she managed to struggle to the surface of the deep well where she'd been foundering.

"It...can't be," she contradicted him.

"I'm afraid it is. If we don't get going, we'll miss the truck, and have to walk to the groves. We'll also get docked a portion of our wages for tardiness."

They were hardly doing their stint as pickers for the money. Still, the prospect of being disciplined by Ralph, Curly and their ilk galvanized her. She was out of bed, buttoning her blouse and brushing the night's tangles from her hair in just seconds. As she washed down an unaccustomed early breakfast of peanut butter on stale white bread with some of the water Mike had pumped, their trailer, with its rotting floor and bare-bulb lighting, looked even less appealing than it had the night before.

You can't let these surroundings get you down, she admonished herself. They aren't permanent. Besides, you *asked* to come along. Making a quick trip to the nearest outdoor toilet, she was ready at the appointed time to climb with Mike into the back of a flatbed truck that waited by the company store.

For Sherry, whose previous jobs as a beautician, manicurist and secretary hadn't prepared her for it, picking oranges turned out to be punishing work. Branches whipped against her face. Juice trickled to her elbows. It wasn't long before she was sporting blisters on both hands as Jolene had predicted. Attempting to favor them, she slowed her work, only to be hounded and criticized by one of the female labor bosses.

The more experienced pickers had packed lunches. Mike and Sherry hadn't, for reasons he hadn't bothered to explain. By the time a lunch wagon had arrived with soft drinks, burritos, cold sandwiches and hot dogs, she was starving and dying of thirst. "A burrito and a diet cola would be heavenly," she told Mike, flexing her sore muscles as they got in line together.

He nodded his agreement. "I can't wait to document what our employer's charging for them."

A careful shopper, Sherry was horrified to learn what their sketchy, barely nutritious lunch would cost. Incredibly, it added up to nearly a quarter of their day's wages. "At this rate," she whispered, "we wouldn't have anything left over at the end of the week to pay our rent. We'd be in perpetual hock to the camp management!"

"That's the general idea," Mike assented, relishing the skinny hot dog to which he'd added an extra dollop of chili sauce.

By the time their workday ended around twelve hours after they'd begun it, the lines at the showers were impossibly long. They decided to sponge off before dinner at their faucetless kitchen sink. They'd just begun another meal of water, bread and peanut butter when Curly sought them out. Undressing Sherry with his eyes, the labor boss informed them Mike had picked up to snuff. Sherry hadn't.

"Sorry, darlin'," he leered. "But the big boss says I've gotta cut your hourly wage in half."

Oblivious to Mike's tacit warning not to bait him, Sherry stared. "You can't be serious!" she exclaimed.

Curly sighed in mock sympathy. "I'm 'fraid so. A'course, I can think of a better way for you to earn your keep than pickin' oranges. Just you let me know..."

Abruptly catching the labor boss's meaning, she blushed and turned to Mike. Unwilling the camp's guard dogs should be called down on them, since he lacked a weapon of any sort, he grimaced in frustration. But he didn't protest. Instead, he simply put an arm around her.

"I didn't want to start a fight, okay?" he explained after Curly had gone. "If he summoned help...or turned the dogs on us... I couldn't guarantee your safety."

Offended and frightened by the labor boss's blatant remarks, Sherry began to realize what the typical migrant was up against. "I understand," she said. "I'll do my best to keep a low profile."

"Good." He gave her a little squeeze. "What do you say we get started on our interviews? The sooner we finish them, the sooner we're out of here."

A bit hesitant at the prospect of approaching total strangers despite her brave talk at the board meeting, Sherry was one hundred percent in favor of that. "Let's go now," she asserted.

Weary as they surely were from their long day in the grove, most of the Brumpton pickers seemed to prefer the out-of-doors to the ramshackle dwellings that had been assigned to them. Seated beside their sagging stoops in battered lawn chairs and ambling barelegged along the informal paths of trampled weeds that ran between most of the camp structures, women gossiped with other women. Children played a form of stick ball. Young people flirted. Men drank and argued over card games.

Separating for greater efficiency, Sherry and Mike made the rounds, introducing themselves as newcomers to anyone who would listen. They asked about the obviously squalid conditions, and what they'd perceived to be substandard treatment. To neither's surprise, each time they established contact, they got an earful. Though they couldn't take notes openly, they made a mental list of people they thought might be willing to testify.

Experienced with infants thanks to caring for Jamie, Sherry could see that many of the pickers' babies and children were in questionable health. It was clear they got little or no medical care and scant attention from their overworked parents.

Education appeared to be another commodity that was in short supply. From what she was able to learn, though a county school bus called at the camp gate each morning around 8:00 a.m. to pick up the migrant youngsters and take them to school, many children as young as ten or eleven years spent their day working beside their parents in the fields for reduced wages. Others didn't bother attending classes because they didn't speak enough English and there weren't any adults around to make them.

Sexual harassment of the women by male labor bosses was clearly a factor in the general pattern of neglect and abuse. Unfortunately, though a number of the women Sherry met were willing to talk about it, none would identify a particular overseer by name, or lodge any specific accusations. If they complained, they told her, their husbands, fathers or boyfriends would be subject to reprisals. Those who were paid up at the company store would lose their jobs. The rest would probably suffer beatings or have their wages docked for minor infractions.

As she circulated, switching comfortably from English to Spanish and back again as she talked with any woman who would consent to talk with her, Sherry was distracted several times by the flirtatious way some of the camp's young, unattached females were hanging around her husband.

She didn't notice Curly watching her. To her shock and dismay, the labor boss suddenly blocked her path as she left a trailer parked several doors away from the one she and Mike occupied.

"Havin' a good evenin'?" he asked, invading her personal space to the extent that she was forced to smell his stale perspiration, the rank aroma of beer on his breath.

She took an involuntary step backward. "I'm okay."

"I notice you been talkin' to a lot of people."

Glancing around for Mike in the hope that he could extricate her from her predicament, she took a stab at answering him. "I like to know who I'm working with."

"That include me, honey?"

It was already fully dark. There were places in the weeds between the trailers where no one would see them. Or dare to approach and earn Curly's enmity. What if he tried to force her into one of them?

"Please...don't talk to me that way," she begged. "I'm a married woman."

Her prim reproach caused him to laugh derisively. "Lots of people is married," he reminded. "*I'm* married to a woman who watches soap operas all day and snores like a freight train. You got your wetback. What does that prove? I wanna know if you thought over what I said. It ain't often we get a pretty *gringa* like you in the camp. If you wanna earn back them lost wages, I'm more than willin' to be your first customer."

Her face flaming, Sherry attempted to sidestep him. In response, the labor boss's grin widened until his entire face reminded her of an evil jack-o'-lantern.

Abruptly becoming aware of what was happening as he talked with a group of men some fifty feet away, Mike excused himself and came over to them. "Anything wrong, Curly?" he asked with a pronounced Spanish accent.

His eyes narrowing as a frown replaced the grin, the labor boss appeared to calculate Mike's strength and find it considerable. "It's *Mister Tanner* to you, *péon*," he retorted sullenly. "I was just tellin' your pretty wife she better shape up or you're gonna find yourself workin' overtime. The guy who used to clean the latrines after he finished his regular day's work quit last week. We're lookin' for a replacement."

Relieved though she was that his presence had discouraged Curly, Sherry complained that Mike had been too easy on him once he was safely out of earshot.

I know how it must have seemed, he thought. Like I wouldn't stand up for you. And that's not the case. I'd have fought him in a second if I'd had to. It just so happens we're in a lot of danger here, and I want to play our cards carefully. In addition, it had occurred to him that if he let Sherry lean on him too much, he might weaken her moral authority to handle Curly. She needed to be sure of herself in order to repulse the lecherous labor boss's advances if he wasn't around to protect her.

"What did you want me to do...get us thrown out of here?" he responded, hoping against hope that she'd catch his drift.

Sherry bit her lip. You'd never have spoken to Lisa that way, she accused him silently. Or allowed someone like Curly to hit on her—at least, not until she cheated on you. Yet, though I'm your wife, you won't speak up in my defense. Her nerves raw from all the stress that had been heaped on her head during the past few weeks, she didn't stop to think that her assessment flew in the face of everything she knew about him.

Meanwhile, the blisters on her hands hurt. And she was weary to the bone. Re-erecting the emotional barrier she'd flung up between them on their wedding night, she washed her face and brushed her teeth, using the smallest possible amount of the water he'd pumped for them, and got into bed without saying goodnight. All I want at this point is to go home to Jamie, hold that sweet baby in my arms again, she thought. If I can hang around in his life—help celebrate his triumphs and kiss away his hurts until he's twenty-one or so—marrying Mike will have been worth it. Whether or not he ever learns to love me is beside the point.

Transcribing his notes beneath a bare bulb that hung from the ceiling via a frayed extension cord, Mike tried not to feel too badly about her opinion of him. They could settle things later, when they got back to Tampa. He could apologize then. Right now, he had more important business.

Though he hadn't smoked for years, he found himself longing for a cigarette. Why the sudden craving? he asked himself. The answer came straight from his gut, as if his inner man had been pleading for him to pay attention. Smoking's an alternative form of gratification, that man reminded him. You want Sherry. And you can't have her— yet. You're too much *hombre* to take her in such a degrading place.

Her back turned to him, Sherry didn't move. At last, Mike had written all he could. Morning would come before he knew it. He needed to get some sleep. Putting away his notes and switching off the light, he removed his T-shirt and stepped out of his jeans. Wearing just his shorts, he got into bed, keeping carefully to his own space.

For several minutes they lay side by side, mutually wakeful. On the verge of reaching out to caress her shoulder and try to explain his seemingly callous behavior, Mike stayed his hand. Someone—Curly Tanner, he guessed—was approaching their window. Seconds later, the labor boss paused outside it and whistled a provocative little tune.

At her first hint of Curly's presence, Sherry had stiffened. A shudder went through her when he whispered her name.

His anger and disgust with the labor boss approaching flash point, Mike forced himself to keep it in check. Where Sherry was concerned, on the other hand, he followed his instincts. "I won't let him touch you, sweetheart...even if that means breaking his neck," he vowed, enfolding her.

Relief seeping into every pore, she clung to him. Seconds later, Curly had gone on about his business and Mike was tightening his embrace. "If necessary, I'd chuck the whole damn mission for your sake...didn't you know that?'' he said.

Shaking her head in denial, Sherry nestled closer, his chest hair soft yet pleasantly crisp against her face.

"Don't you know how much I want you?'' he added.

"As much as I want you?''

Abruptly their surroundings, the ignoble reality of their battered trailer, seemed to disappear, along with the emotional barriers that had separated them. It was as if a gauzy curtain had descended, creating a microcosm of safety and comfort. Within its precincts, their lumpy mattress became a queen's bed, the rough blanket they'd cast aside in their eagerness for contact a sable robe. For as long as they wished, even if it took all night, they'd be blissfully free to pleasure each other.

In that velvety cocoon of night, of cool, moisture-laden breezes and hot desire, nothing mattered but the fact that they were together. Instead of a drawback that inhibited him, Sherry's virginity had become a prize—one Mike believed he didn't deserve but would gladly take, humble that she'd offer it. Though his need for her was rocketing out of control as he removed her T-shirt and caressed the softly rounded bounty that spilled into his keeping, he vowed to take it slow, carry her all the way with him.

Already she could feel the hard evidence of his passion seeking against her. "My panties too, Mike...please...'' she begged.

His soft answer was phrased in Spanish, the language that, for him, had always been intimately connected with lovemaking. "Let me accommodate you, *preciosa*...''

Fierce in his tenderness, uncompromising in the pleasure he exacted from her, Mike stroked her inner thighs as he tugged the unwanted garment from her hips. Her little frissons of pleasure only fueled his urgency. I won't leave an inch of her untouched, he promised himself. I'll make her mine. Setting about the infinitely erotic business of keeping his word, he caressed her mouth, her neck, her breasts, the smooth, luxurious curve of her stomach.

Can this be real? Sherry asked herself as the radiance of arousal claimed her. Or am I only dreaming it? Will Mike and I take each other past the limits as men and women have been doing for thousands of millenia? Become in some mystical way the flesh of each other's flesh? She'd wanted him so badly—from the moment she'd laid eyes on him if she cared to admit the truth—and now it was happening.

As Mike's fingertips adventured further, exploring her responsive lower stomach and parting her nest of light-brown curls, his mouth began a rapacious but loving quest. Fastening on one sensitive peak, he flicked it with his tongue. The arbitrary rhythm he employed only added to her craving. Bursts of longing flowered, like brilliant red poinsettias opening in time-lapse photography. With the speed of light, they connected her erect nipples with the wet, dark place she'd kept inviolate for him.

"Mike . . . oh, Mike," she breathed. "I want you so much."

"You'll have me this time . . . never doubt it," he whispered.

She wanted him inside her, as deep as it was possible for him to get. "Take off your shorts," she prompted.

His eyes drowsy-looking in his anticipation, Mike honored her request. Abruptly, he thought of something. "I didn't bring protection," he admitted in consternation.

By now, Sherry was beyond any consideration of risk, except as a means of furthering her ecstasy. So what if she got pregnant her first time? She wanted to have Mike's baby, the way her sister had. In truth, her body craved it.

Jamie will love having a little brother or sister, she thought. "I don't care," she insisted, brazenly caressing his nakedness.

Chapter Eleven

On fire from the discovery Sherry wanted him enough to risk having his baby, Mike let go of scruples. Though he'd just acquired an eleven-month-old son he'd already come to love, his memories of the boy's birth mother were a source of pain to him. With Sherry, it would be different. She'd never cheat on him, or shame him as Lisa had. If he got her pregnant, he'd shout it from the rooftops—hover over her during the child's gestation like a guardian angel.

Parting her thighs, he positioned himself between them, more eager for communion with the opposite sex than he could remember. A light stroke of his fingertip told him she was wet and ready. "Sure you don't want me to do...what I did before first?" he asked.

Her gray eyes gleaming up at him from a puddle of moonlight, Sherry shook her head.

A flicker of pain accompanied his first thrust, causing her to grimace. But the discomfort didn't last. Wrapping her legs around his and pulling him deeper, she wouldn't let him retreat. You're mine at last, she thought, half-delirious at the sense of completion she felt. And I'm yours.

Without consciously arranging it, they'd assumed an overlapping position, so that Mike rode high against her, and her face was buried against his chest. The contact it promoted was almost unbearably exquisite. Already his repeated friction against her desire had caused her to begin her ascent.

How long they wrestled there, separate beings seeking mutual release and culmination, Sherry couldn't have said afterward. She only knew that the object of their striving would surpass anything she'd previously experienced.

Bombarded with sensation, lost in the exotic wilderness of union with the man she loved, she approached the point of no return in what seemed just minutes. With no experience to guide her, and only her female instinct to rely upon, she prepared by raising her lower body slightly from the bed and gathering purchase with her feet.

The moaning she heard as, rhythmically, she began to knead the mattress with her sensitive soles seemed to come from something primal in herself. Acutely tuned to her response, Mike intensified their pace. She was flooded with arousal, quivering.

Thoughts of the bargain she'd struck and its possible consequences pushed her past the brink.

"Oh...oh...oh..." she cried, jerking with abandon as the tremors took her. Delicious in their intensity, waves of gooseflesh washed over her. They were followed by a heat flush that seemed to emanate from some internal furnace. Tears of ecstasy she couldn't remember crying had wet her cheeks.

Turned on by her satisfaction, Mike followed within seconds. Groaning, weeping, almost praying in his attainment, he excited a reprise that bathed Sherry in afterglow.

Supine, almost boneless, suffused with peace and the total discharge of tension from their muscles, they drifted down, their arms about each other. Relaxed beneath him, immersed in contentment, she supported his body weight.

At last he stirred. A breeze had come up, drying their sweat, and he moved to cover them. "You're so beautiful, so perfect," he whispered, stretching out on his back and drawing her into the circle of his arm.

He hadn't mentioned love. Her hair tangled, the perfumed aura of lovemaking clinging to her skin, Sherry decided it didn't matter. "You're the beautiful one," she attested.

Within minutes, they were both fast asleep.

Though none had been predicted, the rush of breeze had presaged a storm. Awakening a half hour later as it started to rain, Sherry realized that, though she and Mike had turned their backs to each other, they were touching, buttocks to buttocks. Even in sleep our bodies know a barrier has been passed, she thought.

Rolling over, she was about to fit herself comfortably around him when she realized he was dreaming and muttering. Unable to make out most of what he was saying, she caught one word with devastating clarity. It was her sister's name. Mike had enunciated, "Lisa..."

Morning came and with it an end to fitful tossing. Determined not to jump to any hasty conclusions, Sherry returned Mike's kisses. She allowed him to ease the pain she felt with several affectionate gestures. Regrettably, she couldn't still her reservations. Face facts... he loved Lisa, she told herself as they climbed aboard the truck that would take them and their fellow pickers to the groves for another day of labor. If Lisa hadn't cheated on him and she hadn't died, he'd be your brother-in-law. In an even contest, you wouldn't stand a chance with him.

There might yet be hope. They shared a little boy and, if the risk they'd taken bore fruit, other connections. If they could please each other so dramatically, so completely, mightn't a deep affection take root?

In the grove, the blisters on Sherry's hands made picking difficult. By the time the sun was nearing its apex and beating down on them, she realized she also had a sunburn. That old folk song about shoveling sixteen tons of coal, only to be older and more deeply indebted to one's employer is painfully appropriate to this situation, she thought.

Despite her discomfort and the musings she couldn't quell about the name that had fallen from Mike's lips, the morning went well. The women were talking to her more and Curly wasn't anywhere in sight. Then Mike was called away to help load one of the tractor-pulled wagons that carried the mounds of fruit to waiting semitrailers, and Curly suddenly appeared.

Saved by the bell, she thought, when the leader of their work crew blew a whistle to let the pickers know the lunch wagon had arrived. Lunchless because their bread was molding and she couldn't stomach any more peanut butter, she gazed at it longingly. Hungry as she was, she'd be damned if she'd pay the price. Sauntering over as she pretended to get in line with the others in order to avoid him, Curly put an arm around her shoulders. "How 'bout an enchilada . . . for a kiss?" he baited her.

On his way back from loading oranges, Mike was just emerging from an adjacent row of trees. Shuddering at the thought that Curly should even *touch* his wife, he lunged at the labor boss. In the blink of an eyelash, they were trading blows.

Desperate to intervene, but afraid Mike might suffer if she tried to come between them, Sherry had gotten her wish. Mike had defended her, as promised. And it was going to cost them. His strength and pugilistic savvy far superior to Curly Tanner's, he was winning at the moment. Forming a loose circle about the combatants, as if reluc-

tant to betray their partisanship or even their interest, the
other male pickers were silently cheering him.

A chance inspection by Curly's boss and a friend of the
grove's owner turned the tide against him. "I know
you...you're that labor organizer and migrant-
sympathizer!" the latter exclaimed. "I've seen you on television. Remember, Joe? He's the one who picketed that
processing plant in Lakeland!"

Exchanging a glance, the newcomers jumped into the
fray. Pulling him off Curly, they held him while Sherry's
bloodied tormentor got to his feet and tested for loose teeth.
"Okay," he said, his offensive grin returning when he
found none. "It's your turn."

"No!" Sherry cried, letting go of caution as she dug her
uncharacteristically short fingernails into Curly's arm.
"You started this. I'll see you jailed if you hurt him!"

Brushing her aside as if she were some annoying form of
insect, Curly punched Mike in the face.

"You shouldn't be seeing this," one of the women whispered in Spanish. "Or be here when it finishes. You want
Curly to rape you? He's done it to others. Let your man
fend for himself."

As the labor boss's blows continued to rain on Mike and
he was hampered from preventing them, the Mexican
woman, whose name was Rosa, dragged Sherry from the
scene. Risking censure and lost wages to help her, she insisted they return to the housing area.

It was a weeping, stumbling trek that cut across the
grove, during which Sherry imagined the worst. What if
they kill him? she tormented herself.

Tugging her into the run-down cabin she shared with her
husband and five children, Rosa insisted Sherry imbibe a
soothing herbal brew traditionally drunk in her native
province to reduce stress, and secrete herself in an upper
bunk. "My son, Juanito, usually picks but today he has the
headache," she explained introducing a lanky but muscu-

lar teenager who was listening in desultory fashion to a cheap radio. "He'll watch over you. *No tienes miedo.* He hates Curly as much as you do. He won't tell anyone of your presence."

Drowsy from Rosa's herbal concoction despite her fear for Mike, Sherry hid in the bunk she indicated behind the family's piled-up bedding for several hours. Though she strained her ears, she couldn't pick up the sound of any distant commotion. By now, she guessed, the fight was over. Had Mike been taken to the hospital? Or was he lying in a ditch somewhere, with a concussion and broken bones?

Twice she started to get up and look for him, and thought better of it for Jamie's sake. Too many women had been murdered by men like Curly. If he lost both her and Mike, Jamie wouldn't have any parents.

Around quitting time, Rosa returned with her husband and several friends. "Your man has been kicked out of the camp in very bad shape," she reported.

His eyes downcast, Rosa's husband apologized for not offering Mike any support. "We wanted to help," he told her. "Especially after we learned of the work he does. Unfortunately, we have our families to think about."

Horrified by the news of Mike's injuries, Sherry barely heard him. She began putting on her shoes. Whatever the consequences, she'd go to him. More than Jamie at the moment, he needed her.

"You can't go anywhere," one of Rosa's friends warned in Spanish, stopping her. "Especially, you can't try to leave the camp. They'll be looking for you. If they catch you, they'll try to use you to silence your husband."

Half out of her mind with worry about Mike, Sherry wondered if she'd ever see him or Jamie again.

At the bleak expression on Sherry's face, Rosa patted her shoulder. "You can stay here, with us," she said, "until we can smuggle you out or your husband returns," she said, silently daring anyone to oppose her. "You can hide in one of the children's bunks."

Tossed by Curly and his partners into a weed-choked ditch some five hundred yards from the camp gate, Mike came to and took stock of the situation. Night had fallen. He was bleeding from numerous cuts about his face. Both his eyes were nearly swollen shut. His head felt funny. So did his collarbone. His ribs were aching. Still, he didn't think his injuries were life threatening.

Meanwhile, the worst had happened. Sherry was trapped inside the Brumpton camp without him. And Curly was after her with vengeance in his heart. Far from a phone, and painfully aware he wouldn't make it far unaided, he tried to think what to do. Somehow, despite his pitiful condition, which would be likely to frighten the average motorist, he had to snag a ride.

He decided to get started on foot. His odyssey turned out to be a long one, punctuated by lengthy but necessary rest periods and a shambling gait that resembled the stagger of an active alcoholic.

At last a black farmer slowed down and took a look at him, peering at his injuries with the aid of a flashlight. "You're in pretty bad shape, man," he commented from behind the wheel of his dusty pickup. "What happened to you, anyway?"

Haltingly, because his mouth hurt, Mike explained.

The farmer grimaced and shook his head. "That place has some reputation!" he said. "I can see it's earned. C'mon...get in. I'll take you wherever you wanna go."

From the farmer's modest concrete-block residence, Mike called Hector and the county sheriff. A short time later, he was being admitted to Citrusburg Memorial Hospital.

* * *

At the camp, most of the pickers and their families had finished supper. Though some were out and about, partaking of their usual activities, most stayed fairly close to home base, as if they thought the trouble that had erupted during the lunch hour might reassert itself. The fact that Curly had been scarce since then caused some to speculate he'd sustained heavy injuries of his own and didn't want the laborers he bossed laughing at him.

Heartsick about Mike, Sherry wanted to confront the camp management and demand to know his whereabouts. Her savior, Rosa Martinez, counseled against it. They were still arguing the pros and cons when rumors flew like wildfire. Something unheard of had happened. Morgan County sheriff's deputies were at the gate.

After some searching, Hector and two of the deputies who'd accompanied him found Sherry. "Thank God you're all right," Mike's second in command exclaimed, crossing himself.

Throwing her arms around him though they weren't exactly friends, Sherry was interested in just one thing. "Where's Mike?" she demanded urgently. "Is he all right? If they've done anything to hurt him . . ."

Lowering his voice with a caution against prejudicing possible witnesses, Hector filled her in. Mike was in a local hospital, with several cracked ribs and a slight concussion. However, his prognosis was good. He'd be released as soon as his doctor was sure no brain swelling had resulted.

"Please . . ." Sherry swept the disarray of her usually smooth hair back from her face with a distracted gesture. "Take me to him."

"I will. Don't worry." Awkwardly Hector patted her shoulder. "First these deputies want you to point out the man who accosted you . . . along with anyone else who was involved in the fight."

Just then, a third deputy approached with Curly in tow. "He's the one," she accused.

"What about him?" Hector pointed to Curly's boss, who was making a show of being cooperative. "Was he in it, too?"

She nodded. "Someone told me the other man who joined them is a friend of the owner. That he doesn't work here. I don't know his name, or where he lives. I can pick him out of a lineup, though." Her information given, Sherry was allowed to go. Thanking Rosa and Aurelio Martinez for all their help, she accompanied Hector to the camp office, where he scornfully paid her bill. "Let's go," he said, guiding her to his pickup. "Mike's worried as hell about you. I doubt if he'll start healing until he knows you're safe."

By the time they arrived at Citrusburg Memorial, it was going on 10:00 p.m. Exhausted though he was from his injuries and worried about Sherry, Mike had allowed a bevy of TV cameramen and reporters into his room. Gathered around his bed to his nurses' disapproval, they were interviewing him.

To Sherry's chagrin, Channel 11's Mary Murchison was foremost among them. Despite the black eyes, cuts and bruises that made Sherry's heart turn over, Mary was flirting outrageously with him.

A moment later, he spotted her.

"Sher...thank God!" Holding out one bandaged hand, Mike insisted she join him in the glare of the TV cameras. Though she was a mess from head to toe, she complied. After a lengthy hug that did his cracked ribs little good but amply demonstrated the invincibility of his constitution, he introduced her to everyone.

"My wife, Sherry," he said with affection and pride she was too distraught to hear. "She was my partner in the fateful investigation."

Keeping her close with a firm grip on her hand, he agreed to continue the interview, provided they didn't ask her any questions. Before long, his television-journalist admirers had to go. The pressures of the 11:00 p.m. newscast were calling them.

"Are you okay?" Mike asked, lightly touching her face. "With me gone, that bastard didn't touch you, did he?"

Sherry shook her head. "One of the migrant families hid me."

Mike was rueful. "I owe them so much."

Unfortunately, his and Sherry's respite to kiss and touch was brief. Almost immediately, a reporter from the *Tampa Tribune* was on the phone. Approaching deadline, he was eager to ask Mike some questions. A phlebotomist awaited his turn to draw blood.

About to go home for the night, Mike's doctor chose that somewhat hectic moment to check back and see how he was doing. "Everybody out of the room for a moment, okay?" the physician said. "Mr. Ruiz, if you could ask your phone friend to call back later? I'd like to re-examine you."

Hector decided to avail himself of the break to purchase a soft drink in the hospital snack bar. As she and the phlebotomist chatted in the hall, Sherry learned to her surprise that he knew Mike from high school.

"I haven't seen him for ages," the good-natured technician said. "Not since my wife and I ran into the two of you that Sunday afternoon at Selena's almost two years ago. I don't suppose you remember. You were blonder then."

Exhausted from the day's events, Sherry let pain grip her. He was talking about Lisa. Though she didn't agree, she'd been told numerous times that they resembled each other.

"I remarked to Jenny at the time how much in love you were...that Old Mike had finally met his match," the phlebotomist added, glancing at her wedding ring. "I can't wait to tell her I ran into you."

As he rambled on, calling up memories from his and Mike's high school days, Sherry was forced to face a bittersweet truth. Mike had loved her dead sister, whether or not either of them had realized it. In light of what happened later, she thought, it's anybody's guess if he'd have forgiven her. Chances are he would have, if he'd known about the baby.

Emotionally worn down and physically exhausted from her experiences at the migrant camp, Sherry couldn't keep what optimism she had left from dropping through her shoes. I'm not sure I can exist on crumbs from Lisa's table, she thought in desperation. Or settle for lovemaking as a factor of availability. I'm not sure a marriage based solely on our need to provide a home and two parents for Jamie will be enough.

When she, Hector and the phlebotomist were allowed back into Mike's room, she was extremely quiet and thoughtful. Mercifully she was spared a second recitation of the meeting at Selena's two years earlier. An emergency case had come in and the phlebotomist was being paged.

She didn't demur when Hector suggested they return to Tampa for the night so Mike could get some rest. Her lips barely brushing Mike's as she kissed him goodnight, she followed his second in command out of the room. Sequestered in her thoughts, she barely wished Hector goodnight when he dropped her off at Mike's apartment.

Not bothering to wash and change, though she felt filthy to the skin, she drove immediately to her in-laws' house. It was getting late and Jamie was fast asleep. Nonetheless, she scooped him up, wrapped him in a blanket, and picked up what she could carry of his things.

"Mike's fine," she told a distraught Isabel Ruiz, who had just seen the story of their travails on television. "I'll be back for the playpen in the morning, before I drive out to Citrusburg and visit him."

Returning to the apartment, she put Jamie to bed after holding him close and planting a half dozen urgent kisses on his rosy cheeks. "I love you, baby," she whispered as his thumb crept into his mouth.

Her next priority was the shower. Keeping unpleasant thoughts at bay until she could wash away the sweat, grime and degradation of Brumpton Groves, she luxuriated in soap and warm water for at least twenty minutes.

Okay, she told herself, a knot of unhappiness firmly established in her stomach as she returned to the living room with damp hair and a light robe knotted about her waist. What's the drill? Shall I have it out with Mike? Or simply decide for myself how much pain and second-fiddle playing I can take? If I stay with him and we don't talk about it, the ghost of his affair with Lisa will always haunt me.

The way Mike had made love to her in their migrant trailer—so passionately and exquisitely it was as if he'd never cared for another woman—pulled her in one direction. So did her strong feelings for him. Memories of Lisa and the way men had always thrown themselves at her feet sought to shift her in another. The absence of any declared affection in her marriage to Mike hung in the balance, threatening to tip the scales.

Abruptly she recalled a photograph album she'd noticed on the shelf in Mike's closet but hadn't investigated out of respect for his privacy. Now she wanted to see it, scruples be damned. If he's kept any pictures of them together, she thought, maybe they'll give me some clue about his feelings. Even the fact that he still has them—if he does—will tell me something, I suppose.

As expected, though she'd hoped against hope it wouldn't, the album contained several dozen photos taken during Mike's affair with her sister. Sherry blinked back tears as she found he'd kept a copy of the same commercial snapshot taken aboard a gambling cruise ship that Lisa had saved and left behind in a shoe box at their grandmother's house. He was gazing at a ship like that one as we stood on the balcony outside our Clearwater motel room on our wedding night, she realized.

For the second time, she studied the happiness that radiated from the faces in the breezy photograph. Other pictures told the same gut-wrenching tale. Whether they'd been snapped at the beach, outside his apartment as they'd washed his car, or by a waiter at some fancy restaurant, the pictures had settled her doubts. In each of them, Mike had clearly been besotted with his catch. Even those he'd taken of Lisa by herself spoke mutely of his pride and affection.

What happened between us at the camp was proximity, Sherry concluded in anguish. It was stress. Maybe some other woman can help him forget her. For his sake, I hope so. Tragically, because of my relationship to her and the family resemblance people keep pointing out, I can't help serving as a reminder. Each time I hold the baby or share Mike's bed, she'll be in his thoughts.

Going into the kitchen, she helped herself to an unaccustomed glass of wine and returned to the couch. The truth is, she ruminated, sipping at the somewhat flat Chablis, to Mike I'm Jamie's aunt...someone he married to avoid a custody suit and have a built-in caretaker for the baby.

Having secured his financial support and given Mike the opportunity to love Jamie, she'd done what she'd set out to do. Perhaps it was time to retire from the field. The only problem was that she loved Mike to distraction and had come to regard his precious child as her own. Giving them up would be the hardest sacrifice she'd ever have to make.

She jumped as the phone rang on Mike's desk across the room. Who could be calling? It was past midnight.

In no mood to talk to anyone, she let the answering machine pick up. Her heart skipped a beat when, unexpectedly, Mike's disembodied voice addressed her.

"Sherry, sweetheart...if you're awake, please say hello," he said. "You were awfully quiet tonight, and I was wondering if everything was okay." There was a pause in which he waited for her to answer. "I hope so," he added when she couldn't bring herself to do it. "No doubt you're exhausted. When you come to the hospital tomorrow, could you please bring my briefcase?"

Not a word about *I love you* or *I miss you*, Sherry thought, refusing to acknowledge he might feel awkward saying those things to an answering machine. I'm just his secretary. His bed partner. Jamie's baby-sitter. A pallid image of the woman who won his heart.

In a burst of anguish, she made a disastrous choice. She wouldn't get Jamie up again that evening. Or deprive herself of much-needed sleep. Morning would be soon enough to pack his things, throw her own in a couple of garbage bags, and leave the apartment where Mike and Lisa had slept together. After picking up the baby's playpen at his grandparents' home, she'd return to her grandmother's Port Tampa cottage and make plans for a divorce.

Gram's not so bad when you're used to her, she tried to tell herself. Though she never really loved us, we always knew where we stood. Henceforth, her only question mark would be Mike's response to her defection. If she was lucky, once he'd cooled down, he'd see reason and agree to shared custody.

Chapter Twelve

Unexpectedly released from the hospital the following morning when some tests he'd undergone indicated his injuries were superficial ones, Mike tried to reach Sherry at the apartment, FFU headquarters, his parents' house. At his place and at the office, he reached his own voice on the recorded tape of an answering machine. Dialing her grandmother's house, he got a busy signal. I'll have to wait here until she gets one of my messages, he thought in frustration. If I ask Hector to drive out and both of them show up, neither is going to be very happy with me.

By the time he phoned his office a second time, Hector had arrived for work. "I don't know where Sherry is," his second in command told him. "Apparently she was in earlier. She left a note on your desk."

If she left a message for me there, when she knows I'm still at the hospital, Mike realized in puzzlement, something funny's happening. *I wonder what it is.* Anxious to unravel the mystery in person, he bummed a ride with a St. Petersburg computer programmer who'd spent the previous three days revising the hospital's software. Headed for Gandy Bridge, the man was kind enough to drop him at his apartment.

To Mike's dismay, Sherry's clothes had been removed from his bedroom closet. His baby son's tiny garments and paraphernalia were also missing. Flinging himself into the Mustang despite the fact that his head was throbbing and his ribs still hurt, he sped to FFU headquarters, managing to arrive in one piece without incurring a traffic ticket.

The small, white envelope she'd left for him was propped against his telephone. Picking it up, he tore it open and read. Words leapt at him like knives from the page. According to her, he didn't love her. They should never have gotten married. Before a bad situation got worse, she was divorcing him. She hoped they could reach an amicable settlement for Jamie's sake.

As her message sank in, his teeth clenched. His gut contorted into knots. She'd left a note in his office, as if she were resigning from a job instead of leaving him. Though in reality the two situations were quite different, for him her departure was like reliving Lisa's faithlessness. Smitten with Sherry's sister and her lively, teasing ways, he'd begun to imagine a life for them. And come home to find her making love to a stranger in their bed. Now Sherry, whom he'd come perilously close to loving—hell, actually *did* love— was abandoning him. She was throwing their marriage into the garbage pail without giving it a chance.

His body still aching from the beating it had incurred, and his emotions stretched taut with too much stress, Mike saw red. The ferocious temper he thought he'd conquered in grade school rose up to choke him. By God, he'd tell her what to do with her precious self if it was the last thing he ever did!

Dialing her again at her grandmother's, he got her on the third ring. Overflowing with second thoughts about leaving him, she didn't hint at them. "Hello?" she said tentatively, as if she expected to be pasted in the chops.

At the sweet, low sound of her voice, which he could remember too well pledging to make a life with him, Mike savaged her with an untruth that, within the confines of that moment, sounded like gospel to his ears. "You want a divorce?" he raged, adding a string of epithets. "Well, that's fine with me, lady. I'll set the wheels in motion."

She didn't answer. Knowing her, he realized she hadn't been referring to alimony when she'd written about settling things. She'd been referring to Jamie's custody. Instinctively, he guessed it was her softest spot.

"One more thing before you hang up," he added, unaware that she was silently weeping. "As Jamie's only living parent, I plan to sue for full custody. I'll grant you visitation rights if I feel like it...not otherwise. If you make any trouble for me, you won't get to see him until his eighteenth birthday."

Stunned at the depth of his rancor, Sherry gasped audibly. "Mike...you can't mean it!" she exclaimed. "I'm the only mother he knows. He'll be devastated. And I love him so much!"

His answer was hard as nails. "I'm his father," he replied implacably. "You're just an aunt. I'll decide what's best for him."

The following morning, Isabel Ruiz phoned Sherry at her grandmother's house. "What's going on?" she demanded, her worry filling up the phone connection. "Mikey's like a wild man. He claims you're divorcing him, when the two of you should still be on your honeymoon."

Her distress exacerbated by the mounting tally of people she'd wounded, Sherry tried to explain. "Mike married me because he wanted a mother for Jamie," she said. "I wanted a father for him. How could I know it wouldn't be enough?"

"But a divorce!" her mother-in-law exclaimed. "There's never been one in our family. The two of you love each other. I just know it!"

"That's only half true," Sherry replied, a knife of pain twisting in her heart.

Once his anger had cooled, Mike took to parking in front of Sherry's grandmother's house. Hungry for the sight of her and his little boy, he longed to ask Sherry if Jamie's welfare had been her only reason for marrying him. Afraid what her answer might be, he couldn't bring himself to do it. Each time she started out-of-doors to talk to him, he turned his key in the ignition and drove away. The once-burned, twice-skeptical man in him needed to be reassured before he could bare his soul to her. Rueful that their first lovemaking had taken place at Brumpton Groves in the wake of Curly's taunts, he needed to hear from her that she'd wanted it as much as he had.

Grateful that no process servers had appeared at her door to notify her of a custody suit, Sherry didn't protest though, each time it happened, fragile, rekindled hopes were dashed. If she was tolerant enough, she tried to tell herself, he might see reason—and let her continue to figure in the life of the baby she loved so much.

Managing to hold herself together, though her longing to take Mike on any terms was a persistent ache and her grandmother's caustic comments only aggravated the misery she felt, Sherry pounded the pavement looking for a job in her field. She and Jamie needed a place of their own. Besides, though tax accounting might sound dry and boring to some, she loved the work. She also reasoned that, if she could contribute equally to Jamie's support, she might be given an equal role in raising him.

Two weeks later, on a Saturday evening, Hector called. "We're going before the Morgan County Commission on Tuesday evening, in an attempt to put Brumpton Groves out of business," he said. "Several pickers have agreed to testify. Just the same, we need your help. What happened to you and Mike there is all too typical. If you don't appear to tell your side of the story, our case is going to lose a lot of force."

Still horrified by conditions at the camp and the treatment workers there received at the hands of bosses like Curly, Sherry was more than willing to take part. She just didn't want a scene with Mike. The last thing she wanted was to betray her feelings for him.

"I suppose you've heard what's going on with Mike and me," she said without much inflection. "No doubt you could have predicted it. Be that as it may, I'll do whatever I can to help. In return, I want you to promise me Mike won't use the occasion to start an argument."

"How can I do that?" Hector protested. "I don't control him."

"You can tell him it's the price of my cooperation."

"And you say you don't want to argue." There was a pause in which Sherry guessed he was shaking his head. "It's none of my business," he added. "But I wish you'd give your marriage a chance. Mike really cares for you."

I wish I could believe that, Sherry thought, close to tears at a vote of confidence from someone she'd thought disliked and mistrusted her. She couldn't bring herself to do it—not when Mike had called out her sister's name in his sleep, still longing deep in his subconscious for Lisa when he was married to *Sherry*.

"Did you know my sister when she and Mike were dating?" she blurted, unable to stop herself.

Briefly, the phone line was empty of conversation. "*Sí*, I knew her," Hector said finally, with what sounded like regret.

Then you know how much Mike had cared for her, she retorted silently. "Maybe I could do what you're asking if I'd met him first," she said aloud, adding a quick, bland, "See you on Tuesday," before wishing him goodnight.

* * *

That weekend, as he planned his remarks to the Morgan County Commission in the deafening silence of his apartment, Mike kept pausing to stare at the wedge of Tampa Bay that was visible from the window over his desk without really seeing it. By now, the last of his anger at Sherry had dissipated. In its place, a soul-deep yearning had burgeoned to a shout.

It's as if I lost a part of myself when she walked out on me, taking our little boy, he thought. *Macho* crusader and seasoned bachelor that I am, I can't seem to function without them. Of course, he could get Jamie back. Go to court and fight for his custody. Chances were, he'd win. These days, fathers' rights were in the ascendant.

Important as his son was to him now—and Jamie had quickly come to matter the earth—he knew that kind of victory would be an empty one. He wanted Sherry too. *Needed* her, damn it...smiling up at him from a picnic blanket, kissing his baby boy's rosy cheeks, cuddling to sleep in his arms after making love beneath whatever blanket was available.

With every atom of his being, he longed for her to inhabit his life, enter it and stay as if it were a much-cherished house where she could dwell in safety and happiness. If that was love, he'd finally learned its meaning.

When he thought of how he'd handled things, rushing her through a marriage ceremony as if it were a fire drill, abruptly refusing to have sex with her on their wedding night instead of accepting her virginity as the gift it was, and then taking her without protection a few days later amid squalid surroundings, he wanted to smash his fist through the top of his desk. No wonder she's convinced I don't love her, he thought. I haven't told her so. Or given her any reason to think otherwise. What the hell can I *expect?*

If only she'd give him a chance to set things straight. Staring at the bay outside his window, which had turned a milky-blue beneath a gathering haze of clouds, Mike shored up his resolve to make things right could turn out the way he wanted. He'd talked her into marrying him, hadn't he? He could talk her into staying with him. She might even learn to love him for himself.

On Tuesday evening, the county commission meeting room at the Morgan County Courthouse was jammed with pickers, growers, attorneys, farmworker advocates, reporters and TV cameramen as the hearing on alleged abuses at Brumpton Groves was about to get under way. At the commission table, which was flanked by the American and Florida state flags, most of the elected officials had taken their seats. Any moment now, the chairman would gavel the meeting to order. Yet Sherry still hadn't arrived.

Afraid she'd changed her mind about coming, Mike let out a sigh of relief when, suddenly, there she was, slim, frowning, with that special glow she always had despite her sparing use of makeup, pushing her way through the crowd in a flower-sprigged dress. Incredibly, she'd brought Jamie. Dressed in a miniature navy blue sailor suit with soutache braid on the collar and a red neckerchief, his son drew a number of admiring glances. The baby's dark eyes were as big as saucers as he took in the sea of unfamiliar faces, and clung to Sherry's neck.

Pausing to hug thirteen-year-old Armand, the Haitian boy to whom she'd once donated her lunch, and shake hands with his parents, she spoke briefly in Spanish with several of the women she'd met during their investigative stint. At last she took the metal folding chair on Hector's far side that the latter had saved for her.

God, but it was good to see her! And his little boy! Love for them filled Mike's heart to bursting. He wanted to crush them in his arms. Something about the tilt of Sherry's chin warned him not to go for it. "Thanks for coming," he whispered instead, all but forcing Hector to change places with him.

Instinctively he let the baby draw them together. Edging closer, so that his thigh pressed casually against Sherry's through their clothing, he smoothed his son's dark hair. He wasn't privy to the way her heart turned over at his proximity. Or how it ached when Jamie clutched at his sleeve, recognizing him. He only knew he wouldn't blow things again if he could help it.

Though she shifted slightly in her chair, Sherry couldn't force herself to withdraw from him altogether. Inadvertent though she believed their physical contact was, it felt too good. Watching him with Jamie, she realized afresh what a wonderful father he was going to make. If only the circle of his love was big enough to encompass both of us, she thought. And memories of Lisa didn't have to intrude.

Gaveling the meeting to order, the commission chairman saved her from her thoughts as he asked the county clerk to read a proposed ordinance that would govern migrant camps. "As this is the ordinance's first reading, no action will be taken on it for several weeks," he said. "Before we discuss it and get lost in legal particulars, I'd like to call on some folks who've been doing a little digging in our neck of the woods. I'm sorry to say, what they've found doesn't paint a very pretty picture."

The first to testify, Mike outlined his findings in eloquent terms, phrasing them as politely as he could without destroying their punch. "Such camps are on the wane," he concluded. "Brumpton is a horror story that's becoming more rare. It's my hope it, too, will soon be history. When it is, I hope you'll turn at least some of your thoughts toward closer policing of pesticides, and providing decent, reasonably priced off-site housing..."

How special he is...how handsome and courageous and caring, Sherry thought as she listened. I'll never stop loving him. While she was faithful enough to keep him, my sister was a very lucky woman.

Her turn to speak came next. Handing Jamie into Mike's willing lap, she stood to tell her side of the story in a soft voice that forced several noisemakers in the crowd to hush. In particular, she focused on the conditions Brumpton's children faced. "As you all can see, I have a baby son," she told commissioners, keenly aware her role as Jamie's mother might be taken from her. "Most of you probably have children or grandchildren. I don't think you'd want them to grow up in such a place."

Her remarks were followed by those of the pickers and their family members. They told it haltingly, in broken English, yet with immense power and dignity. Camera shutters clicked, TV lights winked and reporters scribbled madly as murmurs of outrage swept the audience.

Finally it was the other side's turn. Grim-faced, the commissioners questioned them closely, adopting the same approach when the grove's owner and overseer testified. Someone whispered that the latter was out on bond, having been arrested for his part in Mike's beating.

At last, a recess was called. Chairs scraped. One of the Brumpton pickers pushed forward to engage Mike in conversation and thank him for his efforts.

My part in this is over, Sherry thought with an aching heart. I hope things work out the way Mike wants, for the pickers' sake. I just can't bear to hang around any longer, knowing I can never really have him, when I want him so much.

He'd returned Jamie to her lap following her remarks and, getting abruptly to her feet, she hoisted the baby in her arms. "Good luck," she told Mike softly, barely mouthing the words so she wouldn't interrupt, and merged with the throng headed for the bathrooms and the soft drink machine.

"Sherry...wait!" he cried. She didn't seem to hear. Seconds later, she and Jamie had been swallowed up by the crowd. Meanwhile, the Brumpton picker had a firm grip on him.

No way was Mike going to let opportunity slip from his grasp. Too much depended on it. The lives they were meant to live, for instance. *Their happiness.*

"Perdoneme," he excused himself, forcibly loosing the man's hold. "My *mujer* and my baby need me."

To his chagrin, Sherry had left all too quick. Though she'd had just a few seconds' head start, he emerged on the courthouse steps without making contact with her. Had she gone into the ladies' room to change the baby's diaper? About to recruit a woman who'd be willing to go inside and check for him, Mike spotted the woman he loved strapping Jamie in his car seat half a block away.

Before she could get behind the wheel of her little compact and shut the door, he was at her side, preventing her. "We need to talk," he insisted.

Hadn't Hector relayed her message? She didn't want to hash out legal matters face-to-face. It would hurt too much.

"The fact that you want to talk...here, now, in the street...doesn't mean I'm obligated to listen," she answered. "I've got to get Jamie home. Put him to bed."

"Not so fast." He continued to bar her way. "Jamie can nap in his car seat, if need be, since this involves his welfare too...."

It was always Jamie. Much as she loved her little nephew, Sherry wanted Mike to care about her, too. "I don't work for you anymore, and I don't have to take this kind of high-handedness," she said.

Managing to stay calm, Mike lowered his voice. "Dammit, Sherry," he pleaded. "Give me a chance."

Her head tilted slightly, she regarded him with a quizzical air. Inside the courthouse, the commission meeting would resume at any moment. Additional matters related to the migrant camp would likely be discussed. Action might be taken. Yet Mike was there, in the street, with her. For whatever reason, she was first on his agenda. Reining in her own anger, she waited with mounting curiosity to learn what kind of words would come out of his mouth.

Resting one hand on the roof of her car, he leaned so close she could almost feel the whisper of his breath. "What I want to say won't take long," he promised. "It's just that I love you and want our marriage to continue. Surely you realize I'd have asked you to marry me even if there were no Jamie, no shared custody to worry about. Although I admit it might have taken a little longer for me to pop the question...."

Convinced her hearing was playing tricks, Sherry gazed at him in disbelief. Could she possibly be dreaming this?

"If that's not enough for you," he added, "I'll take you on any terms you'll accept. Jamie deserves to keep his mommy and have his daddy, as well."

Mellow with the glow of the old-fashioned street lamps that ringed the courthouse square and disturbed only slightly by the distant murmur of voices as the meeting resumed, the soft subtropical night awaited her answer. So did Mike. Stunned at the turn events had taken, she tried to evaluate his proposal. He'd called her Jamie's "mommy," not his aunt. And vowed he loved her. Did he mean it? How could he possibly, when he was still in love with her sister?

"What about Lisa?" she asked, goaded into blurting out the question that had haunted her for weeks.

Mike frowned. "I don't get it. What's she got to do with *us?*"

In response, Sherry blinked back tears. He wasn't making this any easier for her. "When we first...got involved," she stammered, "I tried to tell myself the way you felt about her didn't matter. That the past didn't have to come between us. Then, that night at Brumpton Groves, after we'd made love..."

She wasn't making any sense. Why should his unhappy memories of the way her sister had treated him come between them? Though Jamie would be a reminder, on an emotional level he believed he could put Lisa Hayes and the trauma she'd caused behind him. Asking him to feel compassion for her as the price of Sherry's affection, however, would be a bit too much. "Surely you don't expect . . ." he murmured.

"You're right. I don't expect anything. Not after the way you called out her name in your sleep!"

Mike stared. "I . . . did *that?*"

Her tears spilling over, Sherry nodded.

Elusive though it was, the dream he'd had that night was coming back to him. "You little fool!" he exclaimed, grinning with relief as he tugged Sherry into his arms. "You're crazy if you think your sister has the slightest claim on me. I remember now . . . I was dreaming Lisa wasn't dead, that she insisted I marry her, when you're the one I love."

"Oh, Mike . . ." Her expression dazzled but radiant, Sherry knew with the deepest kind of knowing that he spoke the truth. "Don't you know how much I love *you?* I probably have since the day we met at the university . . ."

"Me, too, *querida.* I was hooked. When I thought I'd lost you . . ." His voice tremulous, his hands luxuriating in the feel of her, Mike drew her closer still.

Their kiss was deep and wild, an echo of the ones they'd shared in a run-down trailer that had metamorphosed into a lovers' paradise. They drew apart reluctantly when Jamie started to fuss. Reckless as he was to have her, Mike wanted their reunion to be special. "I'm parked on the other side of the square," he said, his arms still about her waist. "Meet me there and we'll take the convertible out to the beach. We can come back for your car later. Right now, we have a honeymoon to finish, in case you'd forgotten, sweetheart."

Breeze, lush night scents and Mike's arm about her shoulders teased Sherry with blissful anticipation as they drove to Clearwater Beach with Jamie napping in his car seat.

The motel's night clerk remembered them. "Quick work, I'd say!" he exclaimed, smiling at their son, who was fast asleep in Sherry's arms.

Declining to explain, Mike simply grinned and asked the man to send a crib up to their room. Out and about long past his bedtime, Jamie obliged them by drowsing through a diaper change and several good-night kisses.

While he slept, thumb in mouth, in his motel crib, unaware that the rift in his world had been healed or even that it had existed, Mike and Sherry made urgent love, then exacted a tender reprise of each other. Their second coming-together was slow, luxurious, an exquisite journey to realms more intense, yet more satisfying than either had ever experienced.

They talked a little afterward before falling asleep. Sherry confided that she wasn't pregnant as a result of their love-making at Brumpton Grove. In another year, though, when Jamie was old enough, she wanted to have a child with him.

It was what he wanted, too. "You, me, Jamie and the baby we'll have together someday need a house," Mike whispered. "Plus you ought to have an office, so you can set up your tax and accounting business, while keeping an eye on our son. What do you say we start looking ... right away?"

She'd be able to work at the career she wanted—*and* stay home with Jamie. Have another baby when the time was right. The apartment, with its memories of Lisa, would be ancient history. Sherry's happiness knew no bounds.

"I'd like nothing better than for us to make a home of our own together," she answered. "Oh, Mike... I love you so much."

* * *

In their impatience to set a seal on their reconciliation, they'd forgotten to draw the drapes. Slanting across the disheveled king-size bed where they lay tangled up together, the sun's first rays discovered the golden highlights in Sherry's tousled hair. Weightlessly they caressed the strong arm and hairy, robust leg Mike had wrapped around her.

The dregs of tension wrung from their bodies, neither stirred. Meanwhile, Jamie was waking up. Unsurprised to find his parents happy together, he babbled softly as he pulled himself to his feet. Patiently rocking the bars of his crib as he waited for them to wake up, he took in the sunrise.

* * * * *

HE'S MORE THAN A MAN, HE'S ONE OF OUR

FATHER IN THE MAKING
Marie Ferrarella

Blaine O'Conner had never learned how to be a full-time father—until he found himself in charge of his ten-year-old son. Lucky for him, pretty Bridgette Rafanelli was willing to give him a few badly needed lessons in child rearing. Now Blaine was hoping to teach Bridgette a thing or two about love!

Look for *Father in the Making* in May, from Silhouette Romance.

Fall in love with our Fabulous Fathers!

Silhouette
ROMANCE™

Take 4 bestselling love stories FREE

Plus get a FREE surprise gift!

Special Limited-time Offer

Mail to Silhouette Reader Service™

3010 Walden Avenue
P.O. Box 1867
Buffalo, N.Y. 14269-1867

YES! Please send me 4 free Silhouette Romance™ novels and my free surprise gift. Then send me 6 brand-new novels every month, which I will receive months before they appear in bookstores. Bill me at the low price of $2.19 each plus 25¢ delivery and applicable sales tax, if any.* That's the complete price and a savings of over 10% off the cover prices—quite a bargain! I understand that accepting the books and gift places me under no obligation ever to buy any books. I can always return a shipment and cancel at any time. Even if I never buy another book from Silhouette, the 4 free books and the surprise gift are mine to keep forever.

215 BPA ANRP

Name	(PLEASE PRINT)	
Address	Apt. No.	
City	State	Zip

This offer is limited to one order per household and not valid to present Silhouette Romance™ subscribers. *Terms and prices are subject to change without notice. Sales tax applicable in N.Y.

USROM-295   ©1990 Harlequin Enterprises Limited

Continuing in May from

Silhouette ROMANCE™

by
Carolyn Zane

When twin sisters trade places, mischief, mayhem
and romance are sure to follow!

You met Erica in UNWILLING WIFE (SR#1063).
Now Emily gets a chance to find her perfect man in:

WEEKEND WIFE (SR#1082)

Tyler Newroth needs a wife—just for the weekend. And
kindhearted Emily Brant can't tell him no. But she soon
finds herself wishing this temporary marriage was for real!

Don't miss this wonderful continuation of the
SISTER SWITCH series. Available in May—only from

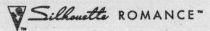

Silhouette ROMANCE™

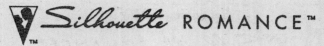

Silhouette ROMANCE™

is proud to present

The spirit of the West—and the magic of romance…Saddle up and get ready to fall in love Western-style with WRANGLERS AND LACE. Starting in May with:

Daddy Was a Cowboy
by Jodi O'Donnell

Jamie Dunn was determined to show Kell Hamilton she was the best ranch hand he'd ever hired. But what would her handsome boss do when he learned she had another full-time career—as a mother?

Wranglers and Lace: Hard to tame—impossible to resist—these cowboys meet their match.

SL-1

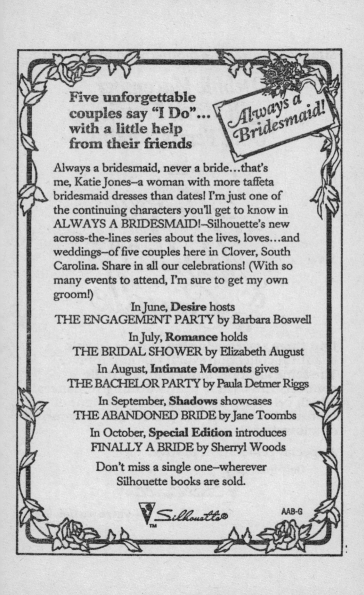

Five unforgettable couples say "I Do"... with a little help from their friends

Always a Bridesmaid!

Always a bridesmaid, never a bride...that's me, Katie Jones—a woman with more taffeta bridesmaid dresses than dates! I'm just one of the continuing characters you'll get to know in ALWAYS A BRIDESMAID!—Silhouette's new across-the-lines series about the lives, loves...and weddings—of five couples here in Clover, South Carolina. Share in all our celebrations! (With so many events to attend, I'm sure to get my own groom!)

In June, **Desire** hosts
THE ENGAGEMENT PARTY by Barbara Boswell

In July, **Romance** holds
THE BRIDAL SHOWER by Elizabeth August

In August, **Intimate Moments** gives
THE BACHELOR PARTY by Paula Detmer Riggs

In September, **Shadows** showcases
THE ABANDONED BRIDE by Jane Toombs

In October, **Special Edition** introduces
FINALLY A BRIDE by Sherryl Woods

Don't miss a single one—wherever
Silhouette books are sold.

Silhouette®
™

AAB-G

MONTANA
Mavericks

Stories that capture living and loving
beneath the Big Sky, where legends live
on...and mystery lingers.

This April, unlock the secrets of the past in

FATHER FOUND
by Laurie Paige

Moriah Gilmore had left Whitehorn years ago, without
a word. But when her father disappeared, Kane Hunter
called her home. Joined in the search, Moriah and
Kane soon rekindle their old passion, and though the
whereabouts of her father remain unknown, Kane comes
closer to discovering Moriah's deep secret—and the child
he'd never known.

Don't miss a minute of the loving as the passion
continues with:

BABY WANTED
by Cathie Linz (May)

MAN WITH A PAST
by Celeste Hamilton (June)

COWBOY COP
by Rachel Lee (July)

Only from ▼ *Silhouette*® where passion lives.

The Loop™

Is the future what it's cracked up to be?

Wake up and smell the coffee, this April with...

GETTING A CLUE: TAMMY
by Wendy Mass

Tammy Shelman didn't know exactly where she was going, but she knew she had to get there, which was a whole lot more than she could say for longtime love Kyle Clarke. *His* idea of a major life challenge was finding the keg at a frat party. Now, after four years and thousands of dollars' worth of education, she had to do more than spend her time drinking beer! And when the worst sort of tragedy struck, she realized it really *was* time to grow up.

The ups and downs of life as you know it continue with

GETTING A GRIP: DIG
by Kathryn Jensen (May)

GETTING CONNECTED: ROBIN
by Coleen E. Booth (June)

Get smart. Get into "The Loop!"